I0418813

Capitol Hill Insurrection

From A Black Man's Perspective

Andrew Beckford

Petcaii Publishing Ltd. UK

First published in Great Britain in 2021 by Petcaii
Publishing Ltd

Copyright © 2021 by Andrew Beckford.
All rights Reserved.

Andrew Beckford has asserted his right under
the Copyright, Designs, and Patents Act 1988 to be
identified as the author of this book; Capitol Hill
Insurrection from A Black Man's Perspective.

This book is non-fiction and where it is fiction
and, except in the case of historical fact, and
resemblance to actual persons, living or dead, is
purely coincidental. Every effort has been made to
obtain the necessary permission concerning the
copyrighted material, both illustrative and quoted.
We apologize for any omissions in this respect and
will be pleased to make the appropriate
acknowledgments in any future edition.

A CIP catalogue record for this book is
available from the British Library.

All rights reserved, including the right of
reproduction in whole or part in any form.

Acknowledgement

Thank you, Yah; The Most High, Yahua Yahushua Messhiach and The Holy Spirit from whom my entire inspiration was derived.

Table of Contents

Chapter 1

Real Talk

L et me make this loud and clear before anything else. I am NOT an anti-Trump person and, neither am I a Pro-Trump. You will see why as you read if you decide to read. I admire many things about this man and appreciate his existence which has created some freedom and eye-opening that would not have happened otherwise. One of the most extraordinary things was that he showed up the USA and the world for what it represents. If anything, his opened bigotry has shown just how hated we as black people are, and it smoked out the racist from every corner and crevices in the States and the rest of the world. These insights are what we needed to move forward, and boy, are we starting to move forward. However, I struggled with whether he is a racist or an opportunist that will use anything to get what he wanted. I am kidding; he is blatantly a racist, but let us be honest, he will rip the head off those same

White people, and they did not have to get in his way. We have seen it through and through. This for me suggest that the White power at the top do not care whether you are one of them, as long as it is about achieving their sinister agenda, they will get anyone out of their way. And to get to the matter of what most have been saying regarding the bias towards the security forces actions towards Donald Trump's protesters or, for a better word, the anarchists compared to the rioters of Black Lives Matters, the BLM demonstrations was overwhelmed by federal policing. However, let us not beat around the bush because the Black Lives Matter is a political movement that does not necessarily have any Black persons in their loving interest.

Now we have White Lives Matter, so we know exactly where all of this is heading. However, where ever it is heading, it will be to the advantage of the Most High as he will triumph. He will use them and has been using them to fit his purpose, and yet they do not have a clue! This fact is what everyone saw, but wait, we have also seen the imbalance of justice towards blacks increasingly across every field. This, my friends, will be the new norm. Make no mistake, though; Trump is just one of the tools being used for a transformation. Let us watch as we see the stripping of the rich and the famous, whether they are Black, White or, Asians because they have already realized that they coming to nought. Some whom the people have made rich, instead of staying and helping their own, are instead running, showing cowardice in every form.

We blacks who cannot run to Ghana, brace yourselves because even with Stevie Wonder running to Ghana, I have bad news. There will be no hiding place for all blacks because we are in Jacob's trouble, and as I continue to write this book, there will be some uncomfortable narratives that I am afraid we must face whether we like it or not.

We all think that Donald Trump was an Ogre and that we have faced the worse injustice under him. But did we? You just watch as the Most High hands move because it was never Donald Trump or any other leader making these moves, but Yah himself moving, and we do not even realize. Back on track, when Obama was in power, it was more or less the same results. The difference was that Obama was very charismatic, and he smoothed us out because he was the first Black male President of the United States of America. However, the build-up of tension was in the making before and during Obama's Presidency. Who remembered the State murder of Michael Brown, an 18-year old gentleman from St Louis in the Suburb of Ferguson, Missouri, on August 12, 2014? May his soul rest in peace as he lay in the bosom of Abraham? This murder triggered the Ferguson, Missouri riot. What about Ieshia Evans? I tell you what;

I shall never forget the perfect stand-off by the lone activist; Ieshia Evans, whose image I shall never forget. It was as if her presence created an indescribable, ineffable space and effect on those riot policemen as she offered her hands out for them to arrest her. Her power was incredible.

Ieshia Evans was standing her ground against police brutality outside the Baton Rouge Police department in Louisiana on July 9, 2016. This stand-off, my friends, was during the tenure of President Obama. My point here is that the anarchy and total disruption did not start with Trump. In essence, I am also trying to tell you that this was far bigger than Trump, and if you think that it stopped with Trump gone, you are seriously mistaken; in fact, it has only just begun, and so be prepared for much worse to come. We are seeing the hands of Yah working, so continue to carefully observe his hands move.

This war is the last stand-off between the Black people (Jacob's children) and the White people (Esau's children); the final countdown, if you may, and in the end, the most ever brutal battle the earth would have ever seen. Jacob's children will not win on their own as their true leader from heaven will win the battle for them. Yes, what we are witnessing is a transfer of power that will lead to the Black people fully taking over and their true leader returning to lead with them. Whether you like it or not, there is nothing that anyone can do about it. Whether you are Black, White, Asian, Muslim, Christian, Hindu, Jew, Sikh, Prime Minister, King, Queen, Pope, or whatever, there is nothing that you can do about this transition as it happens right in front of our eyes. A particular group of Black people will be in full control.

And this will be it for good! Stick a pin; let me just make this clear for all to understand. This information is not to bash White folks, far from the intention of this book. Please know that this is a spiritual war more than a physical one. Spirits do not have a race or a colour. As explained in Ephesians 6:12

For we wrestle not against flesh and blood, but against principalities, against powers, against the rulers of the darkness of this world, against spiritual wickedness in high places

They, these spiritual entities, however, use our bodies to carry out their devious deeds. The divide and rule have been used against every human being through race, economy, and religion, and so it is easy to use the Whites against the Blacks and vice versa.

Many white people and Black people take the bait, so the prophecy has now been surfaced by those who have been wicked from the beginning and have opened their vessels to the spiritual wickedness in high places. Unfortunately, many White people and Black people are now manifesting this wickedness, so it is not all White people or Black people who are wicked. The ones who have allowed their vessels to be used by the devil himself. The chosen wicked White people are therefore playing their parts perfectly in fulfilling the prophecy, and so are some of the Black people. So do not think for a minute that the Black people will be left out. I shall spill the beans on those wicked Black people as well, but wait your turn, I say. I always tell my children not to be fooled by anyone's race, thinking they are good because they are Black, White, or Asian. If you do that, you run the risk of being a victim, even causing your death.

Do not trust anyone I tell them. For every word someone says, I have spoken to them, listen carefully to them and believe them because it is their spirits that they are giving away and, in most cases, not even realizing. I also tell them to look them in the eyes because the eyes are always the windows to the soul. They have been taught well.

Back on track, I believe that it was good that Trump was in power. Being that Trump was called a racist, the publicity and the cans of worms were much more revealing. In the end, everyone had an eye-opening through the media, the system, the police, and the White privilege that everyone knew all along still, it was now even more evident for everyone to talk about and for actions to take place like never before. Trump has done us a favour, but I must reiterate that this is bigger than Trump, much bigger than Trump, and this is what my book shall reveal.

Chapter 2

The Signs we should have taken notice of

I have been to the United States three times in my life, and I must admit that it was not what I envisioned it to be. I envisioned wealth beyond my dreams. The first time I went, I never expected to see so many beggars, overweight people, homeless people, and men in wheelchairs due to stray bullets. Mind you, I went Downtown Miami, Queens, New York City, and the Bronx. I also went to some posh neighborhoods, and the highlight of my visit was the Trump Tower.

What a fantastic sight it was. At the time, I was chatty and curious, still am, but even more so; at this time. So you can imagine me speaking to just about everyone at the Trump Tower, and many of them indulged me. The one thing I remembered clearly was that everyone had something to say about this man.

You would have thought that he was the richest man in the world at the time; well, he was filthy rich, so that is a point. To put this into perspective, this was about twenty-five years ago when I was much younger but very much in tune with my surroundings. The thing was that most of those who spoke of him had one particular word for him, and that word was Jerk. I remember this as if it were yesterday. I wanted to see who this guy was, but it was as if he were royalty, so to see him was just impossible for an ordinary man like me.

The Trump Tower and Trump himself became a distant memory for me until the year 2000. He started to get my attention earlier than 2000 because I remember when he was taunting Barack Obama about his US citizenship, saying that Obama was not a US citizen.

That, to me, was so hilarious. It became a big deal because, in the same breath, many accused Obama of being a Muslim and a terrorist.

I understood why I heard people at the Trump Tower calling this man; Donald Trump, a Jerk. I had to follow up on this man, so I remembered searching about him. I watched his reality show; the Apprentice, and when I saw some of the episodes featuring Piers Morgan and Omarosa, it all made sense to me. In that same show of his, there was always more than one of his participants pitching against another. It was as if he got a thrill from that sort of division. It was in his nature. It was from there that I made some conclusions on Donald Trump. Sure he was a racist throughout his blood; However, when you get deeper into his persona, he is more than a racist for many and at the same time easily seen how many can paradoxically say that he was not a racist. I believe that he is an opportunist who will use any race to achieve his aims and objectives. You see, it was not Trump in action, but his boss. This will become clearer as we get into the chapters. I saw him as a sadist since he did not care about whom he hurt. He did not care if he had damaged a White man, a Black man, or an Asian as long as Trump or the establishment got what he or they wanted. This guy got a kick out of hurting anyone, it was his playhouse, and people never really saw this because lots of money was involved. I think that some saw it in the end, but at all times, it was when it was just too late, and they were badly burnt with their reputation gone down the drain.

He played everyone like a fiddle, but alas. He was played, but to the detriment of the people, and so the question must be asked, who was using him and who were his puppeteers? Subsequently, his supporters, admirers, and voters were all left like fools. Some were only starting to see the light after the Capitol insurrection.

Amid all this confusion, sometimes it is as if the Black man does not exist. Everyone has something to say, but the Black voice has not been heard enough, especially since the Black man has been in the middle of the spectacle. With Black Lives Matter had to exist first, both Black males and females were shot in the streets like dogs by Policemen was like a recurrent decimal, and then I believe someone has to say something, and without filters, I shall say something. I really do not care because I have absolutely nothing to lose. Hey, they got us in a corner, and there is nowhere to turn. Hell, they are going to get every one of us, whether we are young or old, rich or poor, free or bond, Christians, Sikhs, or Muslims. They got us to kill us, so I might as well talk like there is no tomorrow, and then they can come and kill me. They are welcome to kill me because I have been baptized, and the Holy Spirit has cleansed me, so I have no fear of death or anything else for that matter.

Anyway, as I was saying, I am a Black man, and I am going to talk! Let us start with what some of you might call mad talk first. All of this was to come; we just never had our eyes on the ball. I remember about three years ago when we had The Great American Eclipse. Everyone was talking.

I watched the world phenomena. It was on August 21, 2017, to be exact. The eclipse, a total solar eclipse visible throughout the United States from the Pacific to the Atlantic coasts, entirely covered America's fourteen states. The rest only saw a partial eclipse. The most striking thing about this sign was that it had split the USA in half, not literally but by its shadows of the eclipse. I knew that it was a sign from The Most High but I did not know what form it would take in its meaning.

The next full one is meant to take place in April 2024, and I am sure that it will be a reminder from the

Most High similar to the one he had sent seven years before. I knew this much, though, and that it was not good for humankind, although some would argue that it was good because Yah did say that when you see these things, lift your head high because redemption draweth near. There were other signs but not as evident to the world as the solar eclipse of 2017. Nevertheless, I shall explore all the following as I explain all those seemingly coincidences which I shall say are no coincidence.

The signs in heaven, Jacob, Esau, and Rebecca, Esau came out first, and Jacob held onto the heel of Jacob. We shall get back to all of this in due course.

By the way, may I implore you all to go to YouTube and listen to The Book Of Enoch because it will change your perspectives on many things and it will also make you realize that we are in real serious times; every one of us.

Listen! It is no coincidence that technology has ripened at this time so we can all be monitored in seconds, and globalization has made the entire world into a village. It is no coincidence that at this time, there are about 33 megacities of 10 million people each in the world where they have systematically brought us all out of the villages and countrysides into larger concentrated areas to control and manipulate us. Not many of you were taking your Geography lessons seriously, of course, to your detriment.

It is no coincidence that Capitol Hill was invaded at this time which signals the falling of the USA; similarly, it is no coincidence that Donald J Trump was made the 45th President of the United States and now Joe Biden.

It is no coincidence that Covid 19 has happened now, causing deaths beyond our imagination. It is no coincidence that the borders are being closed, and we are being locked in through the narrative of Covid 19. It is no coincidence that the economy is falling with people losing their jobs, and last but by no means least, it is no coincidence that we as a world are heading to a cashless society. It is no coincidence that the last standing Monarchy; the British Monarchy is wrapped in rows of racism and all sorts to signal its complete fall.

Well, think about it. At that time, we had many right-wings raising up all over the world in Brazil, The

Philippines, USA, Austria, and numerous of other places. Do not be fooled though because whether they are right or left-wing, they belong to the same bird.

So let us get back to where we were, Donald Trump. Who was this man, and what was his role in this world?

Donald Trump was born on June 14, 1946, yeah a World War 2 baby, just one year after the ending of World War 2. Let us focus on his mother first. Donald Trump's mother was named Mary Anne Macleod Trump.

She was born in the Outer Hebrides of Scotland and she became a naturalized citizen of the USA in March 1942. What is most notably about her was that she once said to Donald Trump's first wife, 'What kind of son have I created?' This was not in a complimentary way as she was very disturbed by his behaviour as reported by the media. Maybe this was where fake media started from.

Let us also focus on his father. His father's name was Frederick C Trump. He was of German ancestry; however, this was allegedly hidden since this was during and after the world war era, and so he allegedly pretended to be of Swedish origin.

Imagine living on this alleged lie to the year 1980 because he never wanted to hurt his business while his tenants were Jews. Frederick's middle name was Christ, so you see, we must look at this from a religious point of view as we cannot ignore some information. The record has it that in 1973, the government agency's Civil Rights Division filed a suit against Fred because there was evidence that he was not renting to black families. Although Donald Trump denied this, it has been alleged that Fred was arrested in 1927 at a Klu Klux Klan parade.

Again, it is alleged that no one is quite sure if he was watching or if he was a part of the parade. Well, that is what we have been told about his father, but what about his mother?

Well, with that short information, we can get a glimpse of some of the sources of his full persona today. It reminds me of this saying, a man is a product of his environment. With all this information, there are no secrets; why then did we not take notice? Why as a people, have we ignored all this information and not make a stand against such a man with such a history? In my view, this was all because all of these happenings were beyond our power. The prophecy must be fulfilled, whether we like it or not.

Saying that, I will say this much, I still admired him for few reasons. The one thing you cannot deny about him, and that is what you see, is what you get. That does not denote against the fact that he is a liar, but even with that, what you see is what you get because he will defend his lies to the end! Whether you want to pigeonhole him as a liar, racist, narcissist, or just evil, you know what is in the package, and I would rather get that other than someone who pretends to be what he or she is not. I call them actors and actresses. Let us face the truth; everything has been built on lies on this earth, even with our Black leaders. Some of those civil rights leaders are nothing but a lie. That is how they are paid. Before the first broadcasting of the television on July 2, 1928, many of the Black leaders then were on a payroll to be the victims, both Blacks, and Whites; may I add that we were being pitched against one another. And there we had these black and whites heroes being born, celebrated, and even made into statues. Never forget that the black and white man came from the same womb of Rebecca; we are blood brothers of two different nations. Hard to believe but a factual truth.

Well, to spell it out loud and clear for you, without division, those who are paid through the roof can never rule or earn, period. To this day, the same principle applies, except that Donald Trump took it to the highest level ever, and now the demons have been unleashed.

So much now that all is in clear sight. Let me remind you that this is not by coincidence, and although Donald Trump is no longer in power, we have far more and worse to see, and the thing here is that it will not necessarily involve Donald Trump. It is all an act filled with lies, and the real actor is about to reveal himself. It is no laughing matter because it is a matter of life and death.

Chapter 3

We Are At War

Yes, we are in a war, a war beyond the physical, and whether you want to believe this or it is just too difficult for you to understand, I shall break it down for you in layman's terms. Just remember these keywords. Spiritual warfare, world War 1 and 2, and that the Nazis never left us.

Never in my living years would I have thought that there would have been an insurrection or, better put, an invasion of the Capitol Hill. My children did not even know what Capitol Hill was. I had to compare it to Parliament here in the UK. Hence Nancy Pelosi had to be spoken about as I told them that she was the equivalent to the Speaker of the House here in the UK. When I mentioned John Bercow, they understood then.

Hence Nancy Pelosi had to be spoken about as I told them that she was the equivalent to the Speaker of the House here in the UK. When I mentioned John Bercow, they all understood then. How on earth such a thing occurred, I wondered, and then I remembered. It was all prophesied. It started so long ago. Long before any of us were born. This war began more than 4000 years ago when Jacob and Esau were born. Rebecca was pregnant with twins; Jacob and Esau. They were fighting from within the womb, of which The Most High told Rebecca that two nations were fighting in her womb. On delivery, Esau came out first, but as he left his mother's womb, Jacob held onto his heel as if he wanted to come into this world before Esau.

Genesis 25: 19-34

Jacob and Esau

19 This is the account of the family line of Abraham's son Isaac. Abraham became the father of Isaac,

20 and Isaac was forty years old when he married Rebekah daughter of Bethuel the Aramean from Paddan Aram[a] and sister of Laban the Aramean.

²¹ *Isaac prayed to the L*ORD *on behalf of his wife, because she was childless. The L*ORD *answered his prayer, and his wife Rebekah became pregnant.*

²² *The babies jostled each other within her, and she said, "Why is this happening to me?" So she went to inquire of the L*ORD.

²³ *The L*ORD *said to her,*

*"Two nations are in your womb, and two peoples from within you will be separated; one people will be stronger than the other, **and the older will serve the younger."***

²⁴ *When the time came for her to give birth, there were twin boys in her womb.*

²⁵ *The first to come out was red, and his whole body was like a hairy garment; so they named him Esau.*[b]

²⁶ *After this, his brother came out, with his hand grasping Esau's heel; so he was named Jacob.*[c] *Isaac was sixty years old when Rebekah gave birth to them.*

²⁷ *The boys grew up, and Esau became a skilful hunter, a man of the open country, while Jacob was content to stay at home among the tents.*

²⁸ *Isaac, who had a taste for wild game, loved Esau, but Rebekah loved Jacob.*

²⁹ *Once when Jacob was cooking some stew, Esau came in from the open country, famished.*

30 He said to Jacob, "Quick, let me have some of that red stew! I'm famished!" (That is why he was also called Edom.[d])

31 Jacob replied, "First sell me your birth right."

32 "Look, I am about to die," Esau said. "What good is the birth right to me?"

33 But Jacob said, "Swear to me first." So he swore an oath to him, selling his birth right to Jacob.

34 Then Jacob gave Esau some bread and some lentil stew. He ate and drank, and then got up and left.

So Esau despised his birth right. **and the older will serve the younger."**

We are in that time now when you Esau will serve the younger which is Jacob; the same one you called Negro but are from Kings and Queens and the true Israelites because that is the name of Jacob, Israel!

Well, I believe that the black Shemites are now at the heel of Esau, the Whites. Yes, whether you want to believe it or not, the Blacks and the Whites are brothers, blood brothers. Esau was the first, but The Most High also said that the first shall be the last and the last shall be the first. Well, the change is here; the last is about to be the first which has been happening before our eyes. Well, look, the slave owners' monuments are being torn down, Private prisons are being done with, with the stroke of a pen through Executive order, Hariett Tubman (I love her so much) is about to hit the 20 dollar bill. These are only but a few of the never would I imagine these things to have happened. A transition of power is happening right in front of our eyes, and there is nothing anyone can do about that, I reiterate unashamedly.

We must understand that the struggle between blacks and whites has been in play for thousands of years. Its significance, however, started in 70 AD when Emperor Titus Flavius Vespasianus invaded Jerusalem. Many would have thought that the indigenous people in Jerusalem were White people, but this is not true. The residents were predominantly black people who on invasion of 70 AD, ran into diverse places, including Africa and India to the hills. Just as The Most High said would have happened.

The Jews in Jerusalem today are Jews and children of Esau, not Israelites. One of the reasons why I will allow them to hold onto that title Jews is that the letter

J never existed until only about 500 years ago; hence the true ones are the true Hebrew Israelites of Abraham, Isaac, and Jacob. Titus Flavius Josephus documented the invasion and massacre as it happened in 70 AD. Well, if you read Deuteronomy 28, you will see that The Most High told Moses precisely what would have happened to the people since they turned away from him. Well, that started in 1619.

Deuteronomy 28:68

"And the LORD will take you back to Egypt in ships, by the way of which I said to you, 'You shall never see it again.' And there you shall be offered for sale to your enemies as male and female slaves, but no one will buy you."

Egypt, in this case, meant bondage and not the physical place Egypt. This bondage was in 1619.

He also said that after the 400 years have passed, his wrath would be on this earth, closer to his return, and only a fool would say that he is not doing as he spoke.

Do not get it twisted, because it was 430 years that we, the Israelites, were in the physical place of Egypt as slaves. From 1619 to 2019 was exactly 400 years that we had been slaves, and if you have been taking note, you would have seen 2019 was when hell popped loose and when Black people were starting to show freedom like never before!

Genesis 15:13 (King James Version)
[13] And he said unto Abram, Know of a surety that thy seed shall be a stranger in a land that is not theirs, and shall serve them; and they shall afflict them four hundred years;

With so much calamity reaching them was another sign of the changes as the prophecy of 400 years. The Bible in Genesis spoke of that change which will see the Most High's wrath after 400 years since the Hebrews were taken into ships and made slaves. From 1619 when the black Shemites were taken into captivity through the Triangular Atlantic slave trade to 2019, that was 400 years in total. I was able to feel that tense air as if a knife were to cut through it in 2019, and then 2020 hit us like a thousand daggers all at once, not to mention 2021.

Matthew 24:8 is what the bible was talking about when it spoke of birth pain because we are currently in that birth pain, so ten times worse is on its way.

Only three months into that year 2021, and the pressure was hitting us all. It was just as the prophecy compared it all to the birth pain. And almost a year since March, and the pain got worse. For many, it is no longer a recession; it is depression. The virus, the vaccination, the lockdown, and unemployment are impossible for any human to bear, and yet we might have seven more years of this to live with, if we survive it at all. It is all a war, but what is this war all about. I will not beat around the bush. Here I shall repeat, the battle is all about the transition of power from the White man to the Black man, only the Shemite, might I add. I believe that Donald Trump was purposely put into power because they knew that he was the only one with the personality to create all the chaos and confusion that would deflect us from their devious plans. They knew that Donald Trump would play by the script and at the same time do the unthinkable that was relevant to only a national insurrection called local terrorism. He is no different from the Democrats, who are playing the same game; as said before, the left-wing and the right-wing are of the same bird, so we are not fooled. It does not matter what they do; they will fail because the 400 years are up, so their time is up!

So how does this physical and, more so, spiritual war tie in with the Capitol insurrection?

Before we look at this, remember some of the elements put in place all around the world. All these are put in place to ensure that the transition does not take place.

These were just some of the thoughts that came to mind as I reflected on what we are going through.

> A pandemic Like never seen before, yet Some says its nothing but a plandemic

> New York that never sleeps is now most certainly asleep

> Disney, no more magic oh well, only panic

> London has become a ghost town The Queen only speaks from a computer monitor No more country to visit even on our own, we all now wonder where is her crown

> Rome 'The eternal city.' is now alone

- ➢ Paris 'the land of fashion.' is now unmodish
- ➢ United Nations and G-8 is now powerless now they all hate
- ➢ No plane in the sky so how can we fly
- ➢ LIC, NEE and HIC (Low Income Countries, Newly Emerging Economies and High Income Countries) all are on their knees with starvation, only a doorstep away as the borders are being closed one by one and no one at ease
- ➢ Those Godless pastors, leaders, and Church leaders, they all moan about their tithes Churches Mosques all religions too The pastors say there is no more delight
- ➢ Parks Museums, stadiums and other spaces are all but filled
- ➢ Football stadiums and sports events all are cancelled not even the beatings of drums
- ➢ Our own America Got talent Britain Got talent The X factor no longer shows of our own
- ➢ Hospitals for some yet most cannot flee
- ➢ Idols and celebrities are all left alone not to be worshipped anymore
- ➢ And above all, here we in our humble abode

cannot step out and Go anywhere.

➢ And, for those who Can afford to Travel abroad,

➢ Only to be hit with 5000 pound fines,

➢ Crippling the tourist industries and all trades As they ruthlessly force all to

➢ To be destroyed This is the state of the world, many sigh today and, for however long Some say it will be worse, even lasting for seven years Incredibly; at the same time

➢ The Most High is cleaning up Greed and evil being cleansed for all in one sudden move, he swipes while many suffer and die

Yes, it is a war, and we are all in it. Sooner or later, if you cannot take the heat, then you must leave this earth. As cold as it sounds, this is the true reality. The insurrection was a lead and a symbol of the fall of Babylon. Capitol Hill is the centre of power; after all, it is located in the USA's capital, Washington D.C. The minute you attack the centre of any country's capital, you have struck the heart of its power, in the same way, the USA attacked Baghdad in 2003.

Damascus was also attacked on July 15 2012 and now look at Syria. Then there was the battle of Tripoli in 2011 when the National Transitional Council wanted Muammar Gaddafi out, and the loyalist of Gaddafi could not save Tripoli, now look at Libya. Although this was manipulated, this was an insider's attack. I could go on and on, even citing Jerusalem, a significant city taken out. Of course, the Capitol Hill insurrection is no different. We must understand that the word capital originated from the Latin word capitalis, meaning head. It is where the administrative functions are, decision makings are done, and a symbol of control. So when and if any Capital and worse its House of Representative is attacked, then you have attacked the fabric of its security and this is where the physical war as it were intertwines with the Capitol insurrection.

One thing is for sure, the psychological impact will be greater, which further impact the spirit of the people. The world then starts to look at the USA as beginning to fall, weaken, and therefore, it was no surprise that World Leaders from countries you would least expect to have a say had lots and lots to say.

Russia: 'US democracy is limping on both feet.'

Turkey: 'Worrying.'

Iran: 'What we saw in the United States yesterday evening and today shows above all, it shows how fragile Western democracy is'.

China's Communist Youth League: 'Beautiful sight.' All this to me suggests the USA's fall is close, and at best, Babylon is falling.

The place to watch closely is London because when London falls, we know for sure that Babylon has fallen.

How serious should we take the legend of the absence of Queen Raven then? The legend says that at least six ravens must be kept at the castle, or the Kingdom will fall. Well, Merlina, one of the ravens at the Tower of London, has been missing and is believed to have died. Although they need not worry yet as they have seven still at hand, it is of genuine concern because this legend is well thought of to be accurate, and one less is short too many. Meghan Markle, Prince Philip, Duke of

Edinburgh, is now dead, and he seemed to have been the glue to their kingdom, and we have Andrew who has been a thorn in their back, and they must defend him as the public at large scorns him. All these are signs of a crumbling monarchy, and yet there is more.

Barbados wants to become a Republic. They do not want to be a part of the Queen anymore. Jamaica has been speaking for quite some time now about separating from the Monarchy as well.

Many now examine the Queen's medal as racist as it blatantly shows a resemblance of George

Floyd being murdered. It is incredible that only now that people are noticing this medal depicting a White man who is supposedly an angel with his foot on the neck of a Black man. It is only being seen now because the 400 years are up, and the transition of power has begun. Their time is up! Suddenly people of all races are noticing things. There is a sudden wake-up, and people are speaking up with power in hand. Yes, their time is up!

Here, it is essential to be reminded of what was said earlier:

Ephesians 6:12

For we wrestle not against flesh and blood, but against principalities, against powers, against the rulers of the darkness of this world, against spiritual wickedness in high places.

Hence the spiritual wickedness in high places successfully uses the chosen evil human beings to do their jobs perfectly. This means that there are millions of good White folks and Black folks who are safe and far from these entities and are of such not a part of the condemnation to come. In the event, though many innocent lives have to and will die.

Putting this in complete perspective, I must repeat that the Capitol Hill insurrection was beyond Donald Trump. They know that the inevitable is about to come, and so they are in panic, and so they will do anything, even if it means to destroy themselves from within in order to achieve their ultimate goal. This invasion was not from an outsider, but an insider, the President of the United States. Can you imagine, the President of the United States of America?

Chapter 4

Capitol Hill Insurrection Did Not Happen Overnight

A ll that we have seen did not happen overnight. Many are appalled by the insurrection. Many have said that the attack on the people did not happen overnight, and I agree. In clear sight, the attack on the people has been happening for centuries.

I want you to think of the analogy of crocheting or knitting, and for every stitch, there has to be an outcome. The results can either be good or bad. If, however, every stitch you make, there are wrong moves, then the results will be a disaster, and that product will suffer the ill-effect of being completely damaged. In the same way, I want you to think of these deliberate and intentional moves that have led to where we are today.

I shall intertwine everything to show how it has been all linked to what is happening to us. We have already said that slavery started in 1619 and we also should know that just as Deuteronomy 28 have shown, the black people; Shemites lost their identity, their names and people like myself can only trace my past with my slave master's name, Beckford and until technology, might be lucky to trace where I came from since my original people had to flee from Jerusalem in 70 AD.

So I can only stop at Africa, which is not my last root of ancestral travel. However; I can only say that now because the power at be knew exactly who we were when they captured us during the start of the slave trade and that was why it was extremely important for them to change our names, be it by whipping, or even dismembering us; anything it takes that will result in us losing our true identity. Think about it, if we were even less than a dog, then why force your name and identity on the Negro? They never knew that 400 years later, this action would come to haunt them, even though the prophecy of that 400 years was written in the same book that they used against us; the Bible. We can further stitch the disaster to colonialism when capturing the Negroes as slaves; they also captured Africa's and other lands, including the call it their own. They took the minerals, whether this was gold, oil, and everything that would keep them prosperous, but for their future and out of fear, they knew that they had to have complete control, so they did not stop there. They could not afford to lose anything at any time, so they had to ensure that the infrastructure was in place, and one way of putting their dishonest acts together was to ensure that there were wars. Another way, was by empowering another nation; the Chinese and have them doing the dirty work while they pretended that there was rivalry between a supposedly new rising power and themselves. All a game, but for how long can you fool us. Not now, because the 400 years is up!

These wars had to come with lies and deceptions, just like the lies of the slave's identities being hidden and falsified. These wars had to be ongoing, never-ending to this very day. Please understand that you are still stitching because all these wrong stitches are centred on the narratives of the Black Shemites,

Israelites, whom I will remind you that we the Black Israelites are blood brothers of the White Caucasians. Also, bear in mind that the black Shemites are Jacob's children and the Caucasians are Esau's children, and from in their Mother's womb, they were fighting. There had to be something very significant about the black people for them to be getting the centre of attention from the Whites even to this day, never mind if the centre of attention was based on hatred shown by both parties. Again there is something bigger than both of them which shall be revealed as we continue to weave the interlocking loops of wool which at this point is covered with lies.

Harriet Tubman was a true legend; in fact, I genuinely believe that it is correct to describe her as the Moses of our times. Without the Underground Railway, American blacks would not have been the same. She inspired so many to this day with her spiritual wealth. I mean, how many slaves can say that they prayed for their master to die, and a week later, he died?

Besides that, her mission to save 300 slaves and possibly more without losing one of them was not the only accomplishment of this woman, led by The Most High, but she was an armed scout and a spy for the Union Army. If you pay close attention to your knitting, you will notice that even in the 1860s, it was not all doom and gloom because even then, you could see that there was light at the end of the tunnel. The black people were like the dark horses, excuse my pun, but they were slowly showing themselves to be at the top despite the lies being stitched in the most deceptive ways you could ever imagine. I am sure that not many of them were seeing it then, just as it is today. Nothing has changed. But, yes, there we go again, one of the wars in America that really should cause a lot of reflection from the Capitol Insurrection. How many of you saw the Confederate flags being carried by Trump supporters, some calling themselves Proud Boys? All linked into the American Civil war. Let us not forget that the American Civil war fought from the April 12 1861 to the May 9 1865 was all about the economy and social differences between the North and South, keeping the slaves, and in summary, to control and preserve power. In the end, though the Confederates lost miserably, and slavery was abolished. This defeat was not good for the White supremacist, and so the web of deceit continued.

We then had World War 1 and 2. Most people will go with the narratives that World War 1 and 2 were both done to save the country and the people. What a load of rubbish. World War one and two were all part of the continuing battle for control, and within those wars, the wealthiest were at the heart of its manipulation, financing both sides of the war and arming them. At this point, let me say that it was not so much about race, but the White and Black people of the lower echelon of society did not realize this, and many of them both still don't get it. Some do get it completely, but refuse to accept it because their mind-set is still in mental slavery and should they change their mind-set, they believe that they will have too much to lose. Well they are about to lose everything, whether their mind-set change or not! Do not forget that at all times, some White people were supporting and defending their black brothers. However, neither some of the lower echelon of Blacks or Whites realized that they were both pawns in the devil's hands. Actually, some of the higher echelons of society were just as ignorant. You see, from day one, we were just outsiders being used to achieve the devil's aims and objectives. These wars were to ultimately fulfil the prophecy as it is written in the bible. The devil's dream was always to be like The Most High to set up himself like The Most High. In the interim, what he did was give humans the illusion that they too could be like God, so they have always fought each other to be at the top, and the Whites were exclusively taking the bait. Make no mistake about this; the black men have also taken the bait, and as they became free, they became greater victims themselves although some will say that they were authors of their own demise.

It was no surprise then that out of World War 1 came the League Of Nations in 1917. This League of Nations was just one of the outcomes of the war, which meant that the world was getting smaller into a globalised world as they desired. Here we had an International Organization headquartered in Geneva, Switzerland, which was established to monitor and resolve international differences. How cute, this was perhaps a big reason for World War 1, other than the scramble for Africa and the other drawn-out reasons they tend to give us. Here was one of the enemies' first achievements to make the world one; today, we call it The New World Order. Of course, they did not fully achieve their goals, so hence came World War two's birth. Isn't it interesting that The United Nations came about in 1945, just after World War Two? I wonder why? Well, not only was the United Nations born out of the League Of Nations, but several other World organizations such as the International Labour Organization, the Permanent Court Of International Justice, and the World Health Organization, which was at the time simply called Health Organization.

I could get into other organizations, but look at the World Health Organization today to see how the knitting has been deceptively weaved to their satisfaction; never mind the deadly and disastrous outcome for all innocent human beings; Black, White or Asian. Was it not the World Health Organization that Trump had a problem with even withdrawing from that organization. I know that many hate Donald Trump, but let us be honest, his tantrums and criticisms have shed light on many things that I would get to later down the line. All these implementations were all organized with evil intentions from the offset, and as for their unnecessary wars, they were also put in place to achieve their evil goals.

Do not forget that it was during World War 2 that so many things happened that could not have happened by coincidence. I will not even elaborate on them, just identify them. Hitler's annual speech at the Sports Palace in Berlin of 1941 was clear: 'The Year 1941 will be, I am convinced, the historical year of a great European New Order'.

This New World Order rhetoric was loud and clear and sounds like the same as today, except that it is here. I wonder who financed Hitler's regime then, and I believe that their descendants are alive and kicking to this day and are the very ones funding this New World Order today? The Nazis never left us; they only dispersed in diverse places with their sick and disturbed minds, determined to continue from where they were stopped. Just waiting for technology to be in their favour against the world.

The typhus epidemic or outbreak was at its worse during World War 2 and to control the spread of this disease, many Jews in the ghetto were forced to separate, only to end up in the concentration camps and gas chambers. I know that those who survived and are still alive would rather not have such comparison to the present-day situation with Covid 19, but there are eerie similarities, and rightly so, people should be able to point this out.

The great depression was from August 1929 to March 1933 and then again returned in 1937-1938, of course entering through World War two. It appears to me as if we are in a depression now as we experience the pandemic. Too many similarities cannot be seen as coincidences, all leading to complete control.

These situations, in my mind, are all being fabricated and manipulated still; as we look at these knit by knits, we must go into poverty because that is definitely part and parcel of why the Capitol insurrection occurred. Many of those people were fed lies, but the fact that the stimulus package was kept from the people of both the left and the right, while the people were starving, had no jobs, and had no money, people were more than likely to do the inevitable. I shall get back to that, but I must continue crocheting to show that the poverty leading to the Capitol insurrection did not just happen out of the blue.

Poverty has been systematically and strategically made to happen against most human beings as a tool to control the mass and, at the same time, weaponized the elitist who will burn and be tormented forever immediately at their death. How could any human being do this to their fellow being and think that they can get away with it is beyond me? Many people have worked all their lives only to realize that they have wasted their entire lives. Some have even worked in middle-class jobs as teachers, policemen, nurses, and even doctors and cannot make ends meet.

Many of these professionals must have wondered how this could be happening to them. They have done what was meant to be the right thing. They invested their time at University; for some they believed the illusion that education was the real deal, yet for so many, they have been betrayed believing that their time spent on studying and working their socks off, only to die a pauper after they have finished paying off their debt or they end up in dead end jobs or even worse, never get a chance to realize their lives ambition.

It was clear that poverty was set as a weapon against countries in the developing and developed world for mainly the black people at first and in gradual time, all race. Don't be fooled that most Whites are rich, because that is all a lie. They do not care about the race; it is all about the minds so do not be fooled! This system was easily implemented through slavery when you are nothing but an object for the slave master. However, that narrative changed fully after World War 1 when great empires such as Russia collapsed to create countries such as Lithuania, Estonia, Latvia (the Baltics). The collapse of the Russian Empire from world war one also created Finland and Poland; Poland later lost some of its territories in the Second World War to Nazi Germany. The Austrian-Hungary Empire dissolved into Hungary, Czechoslovakia, but since 1993, Slovakia separated from the Czech Republic Slovakia. Other countries from this dissolution included Yugoslavia, now known as Serbia and Montenegro, and this is just a scratch at the surface. They did not only change the

Geography of Africa, but also Europe in order to fully manipulate the minds of the people everywhere. The truth here is that they know that we as a people are aware that we are spiritual beings having a human experience. Therefore, most people will not think their way, so they had to control our basic needs, food, clothing and shelter and once they could systematically control us then they got us. Even though they have treated the Europeans better than their Black counterparts, they have still held down their own politically through communism, socialism and even capitalism, whichever you have chosen, you cannot win. They have however ensured that we are divided by complete hate by using race, religion, and the economy.

You see, the satanic system created lots of poverty out of these wars. You can now see that the poverty and deprivation were not only exclusive to black people because further to this came the devastation of Communism which has crippled, mainly Eastern Europe. Why do I bring this up? I brought this up to show that this evil system's focus was not only subjected to one race, and this was so because we are not fighting a war amongst or against the flesh, but it is a spiritual war. Through these wars, they have achieved their twisted evil outcomes, and the more I think of how people think that these wars were about saving them, the more I boil inward and outwards to the end. Even with the outcome of creating conflict, they established in the minds of people a class system further for the purpose of divide and rule. Their ultimate aim has always been to control us and keeping us poor helps them in doing so.

Whether it is collectively done or fragmented, they always ensure that they work their iniquity to steal, kill and destroy, just as the work of their father satan. For example, Haiti, another country that was held down in complete poverty since Tousaint L'Overture made his country independent in 1804. It is believed that he was tossed overboard by the French as he was tricked into getting on board.

The truth is that Haiti had to pay France an independence debt of 90 million gold Francs and this was on the order of the French Monarch Charles X. 90 Million gold Francs is the equivalent of 20 billion US dollars today, it is no wonder that Haiti is one of the poorest countries in the Western hemisphere.

Countries in the Caribbean, for example, are very poor today, Jamaica being one of these countries. Jamaica, for example, was a Colony of Spain at first until 1655 when the British came and chase the Spanish away, subsequently taking over Jamaica from the Spanish. The British bled Jamaica blind and later told them that they were free and independent in 1962, However, the truth is that to this day, they are still slaves to the British only difference is that they are left without the burden of supporting the country, but still, they rule Jamaica without some of the people realizing this. However, since 2019, that chain is being lifted, even though we still must endure the pain just a little longer, but not for too long. The people struggle in most parts of Africa. They struggle to eat, and they find it almost impossible to get a reasonable shelter over their heads. But these things did not occur to them just like that. It was all created to be so by the very people who would like you to think that they are the good guys. And then you have countries that call themselves rich, showing Africa as a country to be poor, but the truth is that the USA, Canada, and Europe are no different from Africa and other Black countries.

Poverty is rife in the USA. They can't even hide it, and poverty is being deliberately forced on the people through high taxation, inflated cost of goods, expensive and unnecessary medication, and inadequate but expensive shelter.

You work to pay the bills and costly rents in the projects in the States or the Estates in the UK, and yet, they both have familiar entities such as crime, drugs, murder, and the substandard buildings putting peoples' lives at risk such as the Grenfell Towers in North Kensington; London where 72 people were burnt alive all due to the cladding of the blocks which added to the extent of the fire. Again, bear in mind that seven of those who lived in that building were White, thirty-two from the Middle East and North Africa, and that should make you realize that about 61 percent of the remaining deaths would have been Blacks. Not looking good there. When they want to oppress the people more in these same areas, gentrification kicks in, and before you know it, you are kicked out of the site just like that. As if that is not enough, people are dying from stress leading to all sorts of incurable diseases such as diabetes, high blood pressure, and the list goes on.

The ones who claim to be rich, you do not want to see how they got their money, in fact, even the ones who got money legitimately are usually better off due to the oppressive persecution of others. Again, we are all in this matrix, and the matrix is there to kill, steal and destroy. Overall, though, there is one main aim, and that is to control the mass fully. All is being put in place to frustrate the people and to make them powerless. It is no wonder then that the chickens have come home to roost and that, in my mind, was what has happened at Capitol Hill on January 6, 2021. I know that many would instead look at the unfair treatment of the members of Black Lives Matter compared to the blind eye to the White people who rioted and marched in Capitol Hill. I would like you to look at the fact that both parties who have been rebelling and rioting were black and white people.

However, you want to view it, they were people, and both the blacks and the Whites were angry and hurt at a system that has played them for thousands of years, even more so, the Black race like never since they left Egypt only to return to Egypt a second time in bondage. At the same time, they were both pawns in the elite's hands being pitched against each other. Pitched against each other because do not believe that the founder of Black Lives Matter suddenly had an epiphany and Black Lives Matter suddenly appeared. Of course this was all part of the elitist creation to do what they do best; divide and rule. However, it is good because it could never have happened if it were not the Most High's will and it will work for his good and therefore everyone's good as well.

The most hurtful thing about all of this was that race was used as the primary weapon against both people, no different since the dawn of time. To summarize this chapter, the 1% elites are mainly White people, but they do not care at all. As long as they achieve their goals, even if it means killing their own. They know that their time of rule is over and now they are prepared to kill all, and, because all are realizing that we are all spiritual beings not being defined by race, the 1% will now kill to maintain that power, and, by the looks of it they appear to be winning because they are getting the black people where they want them. Yes, the focus for them must be the blacks, even if it means giving a few gullible Blacks an offer of wealth that they can never refuse and then use that same new-formed wealth to roast them to death, they will and are doing just that. Many are now waking up, but still they are not fully awaken, but believe me when I say, they must fully wake up fast, otherwise, no flesh will be left on the earth as Yah himself said.

Chapter 5

More Knitting

Not to patronize anyone, but there might be few who would see the previous wordings as far-fetched as they might ask, what does Haiti, Jamaica, The Baltics, and even slavery have to do with the Capitol insurrection? However, we must understand that the idea of a country is non-existent. The USA does not exist anymore. At least not in the minds of that small percentage who call themselves elites. If you have been knitting well, then you would have seen that nothing happens in isolation anymore. Everything that happens is connected to change and to control us all, and it does not matter where you are in the world. We are all interconnected and of such, whatever happens anywhere in the world has some relevance to their intentions of affecting everyone regardless of our race, creed, or social status in life. You see, change is here and these changes are not necessarily what the elites want. The narratives have changed with technology in place. The elites will therefore bring change to us as well in order to hold on to their power, and therefore gimmicks such as the Capitol Insurrection was just one of the gimmicks played.

They aim to keep us down at all costs, and in this knitting, we must continue to look at how they have used poverty to control us and divide and rule. After World war two another tool that was used to keep the poorer countries down was the International Monetary Fund and the World Bank with the primary intention to 'restore Europe.'

These organizations, under the guise of helping developing countries, raped and murdered the LIC (Low Income Countries) with the debt repayment plan alone, farming subsidies forced to be cut by these devils in many African countries, and if you look at many African countries today, their foods are replaced with GM foods and seeds which are of no value. The people are forced to remain in poverty, which never stops, even to the locality of the people in rich countries. I tell you, there is no escape for anyone. The people in the rural areas have been forced to move in the Cities, and for many, they thought that this was good, however for many, they were caused by the push factors of no jobs, poor transportation, lack of hospitals, or poor health care, lack of housing, not enough schools and the list goes on. The people then are forced to the Cities to the point where there are Megacities with up to 10 million people and what the people have ran from in the rural areas turns out to be worse in megacities such as New York.

Ghettoes and I shall not repeat all the other atrocities that follow. Only to say that the successful manipulation of the people, and treating them like Cattle at the same time was all about forcing the population in one place so that they can monitor them and control them like they have never done before.

As they get us where they want us, followed with attacks with the poor air quality, Frankenstein food that only makes us sick with diabetes and all sorts, works us to the bones with little to no pay, and in the process, they infringe on our times to the point where we have not got a life. Those who want to worship just have not got the time; those who want to look after their children have not got the time. Those who wish to attend to their beloved wives or husbands have not reached the time. They got us now, and with the help of the television, the games, and social media, they now control our minds like never before. Don't worry if they did not get your children through these mediums; they got the schools to indoctrinate your children's minds from the get-go.

People realize all of this, but they are helpless because they have become dependent on the system whether they are working or on social welfare.

The worst for me has been how they have destroyed the family to the core. These people, that is, the one percent, got it all organized to destroy the family. Let us continue to do their horrible knitting. Well, from the beginning, they got you to move to the Cities. Difficulties in getting a job mean that both parents must work.

Women's liberation in the 70s was a great move, and I believe that it helped women to be independent, but many women will also say that it took them from their family and children. However, as time went by, the men became insignificant to women, especially if they were no longer putting the goods on the table; it became a competition and a division. That, however, never stopped society from treating women as inferiors because to this day the gender inequality is a disgrace. Children were seeing less of their parents now, and those who could not afford the economic oppression had to either give up their children to foster care or the social services were now well armed to take your children. For the Black family, it was worse because the Women were now becoming more empowered while the men were becoming emasculated. It has gotten so bad now that successful Black women are most likely to be single and the only thing that they are married to is their jobs. In Japan, this culture is literally killing the country, so their system has been very effective throughout.

There was also religion used wherein many Catholic communities became non-existent to prevent that dreaded embarrassment to the family. As if that was not enough, the television slashed the time from the family, and now we have superior gadgets that take your children away from you, and if you dare try to save your children, do not forget that social services are well-armed.

The type of humans that we have developed through this system of destroying the children's minds can only mean one thing. A society that is now more vulnerable with a lack of real education and subsequently little hope for a good job or sustainability. This has made them easier to be controlled, and that is what the elites have always wanted. They think that they have gotten what they wanted, but wait, not so fast; the race is not for the swift, but for those who endure to the end!

In the black communities, the churches have been used to destroy the minds of the people. The pastors in the majority have used The Most High's name in vain to get the big houses, luxury cars, and some even bought their private planes. While they are stealing from the people in The Most High's name while the people are starving, some resort to stealing, some to drugs, and many have taken their own lives.

You enter into the church communities, and you see the people's poverty, yet they are the same ones giving these pastors everything. You see, all these things were systematically put in place to control the people. You may ask, how can the system be blamed for this? The Church and other religious bodies are exempted from paying tax, so the system has empowered them right there.

The government endorses the Church as politics, and the Church increasingly mingles. The media advertise the Church so much that it is just not funny anymore. With all said and done, the people feel it and yet there is more to show just how much pain the people have faced. They can take so much and no more, and so it has reached boiling point, and so we have had demonstrations, riots, deaths, and then finally Capitol Hill insurrection. I know that Capitol Insurrection was all White people rioting, but it was all due to manipulation and the control of the minds. If all these circumstances as described before with the divide and rule as well as ensuring poverty amongst the mass, then this insurrection of Capitol Hill would never have happened, neither would there have been Black Lives Matter.

Let us examine the demonstrations and riots of Black Lives Matter and Trump's people to see if we can see the parallel between the causes of what was described by myself as to the reality of the cause of these riots.

Black Lives Matter protest started with incidents of police brutality and all racially motivated violence against black people. The social injustice and poverty faced by Black people over the centuries had taken its toll, so the hashtag black lives matter started in 2013.

I remember when George Zimmerman was acquitted in that same year for the shooting; I called this murder; murder of Trayvon Martin because there was no other words that could have been used. I was so angry. I could not believe what I read, and for some reason, I thought there was no hope when something like this could have happened during the Presidency of the first Black President of the United States of America.

The death of Michael Brown in 2014 caused the Black Lives Matter movement to rise again. It was, however, the murder of George Floyd 'I can't breathe' on May 25, 2020, by Minneapolis Officer Derrick Chauvin brought Black Lives Matter to international recognition. I remembered watching the funeral service for George Floyd, and I will not be ashamed to tell you that I cried like a man. I was in real pain, so it was of no surprise that under the umbrella of Black Lives Matter, there were 15 to 26 million people who took part in the 2020 Black Lives Matter movement.

Can you see the link to the development of the Black Lives Matter to the leading up to the Capitol Hill insurrection? While all of this was happening with Black Lives Matter, there were push backs with the right-wing movement and the die-hard racist.

There were push-backs slogans like 'All Lives Matter'. There were push backs with the likes of Trump calling Black Lives Matter a symbol of hate. You could see the old tricks at play yet again. All this was leading to greater social tension between Black people and White people to the point where many thought that a racial war was imminent. However, this was by no means a coincidence. All this was a part of the game to a greater divide and, in so doing, having greater control because this is how the elites roll. You should never forget that all of these were pushbacks because they knew that their power of control was slipping. They had to create stories to keep that control in place. All the tricks in the book had already been exhausted, so other stories had to be formed. The apartheid system had already ran its course, the civil rights movement was now stale, so fresh ideas had to be displayed. Now the gloves were coming off and so the police brutality and established organizations such as BLM and now WLM had to come in play. The pushbacks are not working though, so they had to get even more brutal. The virus, the masks, testing, lockdowns were now the brutal 'new' and norm and if you think that was bad, you wait and see as time progresses.

In the interim, the same as usual, black people were being shot like dogs in the streets. It was horrible how these policemen were legally murdering humans in broad daylight. Remember that all of this was built up over the 400 years and never forget as you read that the 400 years means that Esau's children's time is up and the ones at the top knows this so as the bible said, this is Jacob's trouble. They will be coming for the Black people, particularly, the Shemites.

This time they were not killing the black men only, but now they were shooting the Black women like dogs. Women like Ms. Breonna Taylor have been murdered, and since 2015, police in the USA have killed 250 black women. Eighty-nine of them were killed at their homes, as they did to Ms. Breonna Taylor. When you see that the women are being killed like that, you know that the 400 years is up. In the George Floyd protest alone, more than 19 people were killed, and more than 14,000 people were arrested. I will use that protest alone to measure against the Capitol Hill Insurrection. People have had enough, I say people, because many White people are tired of this as well, and increasingly, people know that race is being used as a means of power and control. The White leaders are losing their grip on power, and so they have become desperate now. When 67 percent of the American public supports Black Lives Matter, they know that someone is losing their control. If only they could use a magic wand to stop all the races from coming together and team up against them. Hence Donald trump is very important to play his role for them.

Yes, the support for Black Lives Matter has since dwindled to 55 percent, with fewer supporters from Latinos and White people, but the movement still has a place on the forward movement of Black people. They are needed because there is a legal genocide against Black people, In the States and around the world. In the States, more than five police killings per 1,000,000 are in the States of Nevada, Arizona, New Mexico, California, Colorado, and Oklahoma. In the same breath, 4 – 5 police killings per 1,000,000 are committed in Maine, West Virginia, Arkansas, Montana, and Wyoming. Now, if this is not genocide, then what is it then?

This injustice will continue and even get worse as they continue to lose their grip on power. The enemies will continue to use their main ingredient of control through conflicts and hate.

Now let us examine the protesters at the Capitol Hill Insurrection. The main reason behind the protest was to reverse the results of the 2020 election. Donald Trump was accused of inciting the protesters against the certification of Biden's victory in the Presidential election. There were hundreds of protesters with people of all class. Policemen were involved, politicians, the poor, the rich, the young, and the old. Most Whites with a few token Blacks, perhaps one or two. How many people died? 5 people died, and 179 were arrested. If you look at the cause for the protest and the total figure of death, you should see the disparity by a mile. Compare 19 deaths at the hands of police at the George Floyd protest and 19000 and more arrest compared to 5 deaths, not all of the police's hands if I might add and 179 arrested and then you can see that this is genuinely Jacob's trouble.

This level of injustice was not only to incite rage amongst the White people but to also have the Black people seething with fire coming from their heads. This was to engulf the entire nation and world with a wrath you could ever imagine. It was a complete set up to ensure divide and rule but more so, to create a distraction like you could ever imagine. This dilemma is why it is essential for unity amongst the children of Jacob more than any other time. I believe that never since the beginning of the creation of this earth will we see so much trouble amongst our people. Why? Because worryingly, there will be even greater desperate measures from the losing hands and the transitional move of worldwide power, and believe me when I say that all races are at risk at this stage.

No race is safe, and this is why Blacks, Whites, and Asians need to unite, but they know that this will not happen, and that is why we as humans are doomed. That transition will not see the daylight until the bitter end of the Black man hunted as we have never been hunted before. It will be so bad that we will wish that we were facing the sufferings of the slaves since 1619 instead of what is to meet us all. This is why, every Shemite, must now unite and come together because after all is said and done, we only have our own to rely on now more than any other time. When the other nations cannot use you anymore to get their next meal on the table for themselves and their family, they will be coming after us and it will not be a good look. Imagine the Chinese, Asians, Whites and other Blacks separate from us coming after us. Where will you turn? Where will you run? We are best running to our own and that is what will happen.

Chapter 6

Now let's lay the Bricks

We will move from the crocheting to the laying down of the bricks. Now I am at the stage where I am about to give you a dose of the red pill. Not many have already liked what I have said in previous chapters but, I will say that almost none will like what I am about to say. You see, the Black Lives Matter and the White Supremacy movements both point fingers at each other, but if truth be told, the White race has been the catalyst for the most vicious system that we currently live in. Their system can only be compared to hell and if this is not hell, then I certainly do not want to see hell. I have never appreciated this system and I am sure that I can speak for my other Black brothers and sisters who were never sell-outs. Saying that, the Blacks have not been all innocent and in time I shall show just that. The Capitol Insurrection and the Black Lives Matter movement have come about due to insecurity, injustice, and all that have come about through the implementations of evil that have been bourne out of the quest for power and control. The one thing that must be stated and that is the love of money has always been the source of this evil. The founder of Black Lives Matter is now a millionaire; I wonder who paid her or where did all that sudden wealth come from. How is it that she came out unscathed and worse living amongst the rich White folks now? The truth though is that most of us already know the evil that the White system has created, but too often, we are either not aware or we have chosen to ignore the other side of the darkness. Not today!

I am sorry but, I will start with my own brothers here, because, like it or not, our Black brothers do have a lot to answer for when it comes to where we are today.

Sure there are very noble Black brothers and sisters when it comes to fighting for their other black brothers and sisters. In fact, these Black brothers and sisters will die for our cause to free and help another brother and sister. The problem though is that there are few of them. Few of them such as Harriet Tubman. Fred

Hampton is another whom I would vouch for as a sincere civil rights leader who could never be described as a sell-out and to me the hero for his people. The truth of the matter is that most of the sincere heroes, you will never know because they work underground without detections.

If I am to be true, I find it difficult to name anyone other than Harriet Tubman because many who appear to be fighting for our cause behind closed doors are nothing but sell-outs. When you see them with the abundant wealth and monuments or statues being built of them, those are sometimes the signs of them being sell-outs; You see, they are the heroes to that one percent because they have done their jobs behind the closed curtains to sell us out for thirty pieces of silver. They are the ones who you will see on television being made into gods and what we currently call celebrities.

The few who are fighting for the freedom of humans, be it Blacks or Whites because when you fight for the freedom of blacks, you are indirectly helping to set other nations free; but these few are the ones who you hear little or nothing from. You hear nothing from them because they are working quietly or they are murdered on a daily basis.

Let us focus on the black sell-outs one by one. Black sell-outs such as the overrated hip hop singers and rappers have been on hire for decades to send out the destructive messages through the same media owned by the same historical enemies to promote drugs, perverted sexual behaviour that has negatively changed the positions of black males and females responsibilities, and not to forget the increase of crime including murdering our own race.

This betrayal by our own has been further perpetrated with the black images that they show with the bling-bling of chains, gems, expensive cars, and houses that ultimately go into the pockets of the enemies who laugh at our demise and destruction. Not to be outdone by the dance hall, kings and queens who have sexually and violently distorted the minds of our children and young adults; It has become such a household now that young recruits in their millions line up to achieve or to attain the new 'wealth.' The music is then transported to some of these black Islands and countries. Being the capital murder countries of the world. One of them with less than 3 million people but per capita, the murder capital of the world

Disgraceful, I say, and the ones with blood on their hands are not easily detectable as those who pulled the triggers. The cycle continues like a never-ending carousel. In the interim, the influx of cocaine and heroin floods the black communities as if it were the era of Ronald Reagan deliberately drowning the said communities with the enemy's killer drugs.

If a black leader such as Martin Luther King dares to raise his head up to prevent this, like a shot marker, his brain is targeted, and his blood-splattered.

Is it no wonder that the same enemy invests billions more in the actors, singers, and athletes to showcase their advantage to destroy us to completion. Is it no wonder that they have upped their games to include games and social media to distract us further and, in the event, destroy us all. The problem here though, is that the same technology is also being used to make more and more like-minded people, regardless of race and class meet up and, subsequently played against the core of their aims and objectives. Do not get it twisted, though, because they are very much aware that we are not defined by our race nor our wealth. They are the ones who have created that illusion for us through their elaborate divide and rule schemes. Consequently, they devised a plan to put us in a corner using that same technology to track and trap us. They have had that in the pipeline for centuries. They now believe that this is the time to have us locked and keyed, and boy have they got us all.

The other sell-out has been the Church. You got that right, the church. I have said it before, but I shall reiterate because they have been the biggest sell-outs against black people. Do not forget that when the slave master branded Blacks on their backs, forehead, and anywhere as they pleased the brand on their bodies marked C of E; Church Of England, because they invested and owned slaves.

The Catholic Church, of course, was the backbone of the slave trade. I find it astounding that our black pastors have not only picked up from where these traditional churches continued but have gone to a more sinister route of slavery of their black brothers and sisters. Bleeding their black parishioners out of their hard-earned money is slavery because they are working for them with nothing in return for the community's development. How often would you find these pastors speaking against the rappers, hip hop singers, dance hall songs, fathers and mothers who neglect their children by their reckless behaviours, the preys that they are faced with by the society at large? I could go on. Most of these pastors only use God's name in vain to make money, but now their time is up! The 400 years is up! Look at them now; they cannot go into the massive buildings and steal from a massive audience. Lockdown has been doing so well against them, and rightly so.

Where shall they run now because there is a lot on their conscience as they reflect, but it is too late now, and if they think it is bad yet, you wait and see as the situation worsens? The Church and Politics have almost become one these days, that it has become difficult to separate the two.

All these were all products of a system by the children of Esau to control us, and they succeeded, but their time is up, and they know it. We will know it as well because the times are changing, and it is affecting everyone. Some will probably die without understanding the changes, but for the most part, no matter how slow you are, you will realize that the White rulers' time is up. It is Jacob's time now. so everyone who were our enemies, Black, White, or Asians, will have to flee. As for our own who have betrayed us, a double portion of consequences awaits you!

Chapter 7

The Hate Is Real With Full Control In Mind

I am sure that as a Black man in the UK for more than 20 years, all the way from more than 8000 miles, Jamaica, I have encountered racism many times without realizing it. For the most part, it has been subtle, almost unrecognizable, until February 2020 at a Secondary School I taught at in the Borough of Waltham Forest, London. For the first time, the racism was so blatant, and while one has said that it was not racism, but due to the culprit feeling threatened by my abilities, I disagree; however, never mind my experience, I shall show that racism and hate are real, but not without reasons. The crucial points that must however be shared are as follows:

Black men (Jacob's children) have never perpetuated hate to the same extent towards the White men as the White men (Esau) have done.

Well, the Black men on the other hand never had the power or may I say never had the persona to show such hatred towards his White brother. Ironically, the black men have shown incredible hate towards their own, but we will see why it is not always as it appears. The hate for the Black men was clearly shown through the Capitol Insurrection since it was all about the desperation of holding onto power. The Black men were at the centre of this insurrection because both the left and the right wanted to hold onto power. Both sides are fighting to keep that power, and they know that the Black men are in waiting to take complete control. Never in my life have I seen these White people so confused, and if they believe that the confusion is over, they are bound to be dumbfounded as the birth pain increases. As the desperation increases, the hate against the Black man will increase to the point where it shall be unbearable. With the increase of hate, the increase of pain is shown with unimaginable death amongst our people. Things will become clearer to every man as already, we are seeing that the Capitol insurrection was all linked to hanging to White power and by any means necessary and subsequently exposing their lies and deep-rooted hate from the day our blood brother; the Caucasian, was in Rebecca; our mother's womb.

The Great Civil war of 1861 that lasted for four years, was also built on complete hate against Jacob's children, but what is about to happen, the Civil war of 1861 will have nothing on what is to come. However, let us look at some of the Civil war developments to understand that World War 1 and 2, the Civil war, and so on never happened in isolation, but only as a means to achieve their sinister agenda. From the Civil war alone, 20% of the White males from the South of the USA were wiped off from the face of this earth, gone forever, many to that place of torment that they never knew existed because many of those fools lived thinking that life on earth ended there without a God and for many of them who believed that there was a God, it was always a false god that they believed in and many, blatantly held satan as their own. You might wonder why refer to World War one and two and the Civil War so often. Well, the Yah we serve has proven over and over that he is still in the midst of our battles, although we have left him, and still we do not realize. We have seen how he has fought the battle for us in the Civil war creating incredible opportunities

for the black people. That was freedom and independence. He used Harriet Tubman, and she never claimed responsibilities for her success in the freedom of all those slaves, instead, she gave that honour to our God. How can you not love her? In the same way, World war 1 was used for sinister agendas for the development of the new world order; Yah used it to create unimaginable opportunities for the Black people; particularly those to the North because out of that war came the increase of industrialization, the need for the building of weapons and all sorts, so the man power was needed and subsequently, Black people were employed like never before, and they were able to be more independent with the payments like they have never received before.

The USA never learned its lesson, the North-South divide remained intact, and if you asked me, it only got worse as the same minds of hate have moved from state to state. All culminated on Capitol Hill's step with one desire, and that was to change the course of history. Now, for those who thought that these White people were indispensable and untouchable, you had better learn fast because soon and you will be wondering how low have they come to naught, nothing. It is written to be so, so do not be surprised. For now, it remains true for Black people that the demand to be seen as equal citizens to just about everyone is still the cry even before the 1864 Civil War.

In the same way, there was always a tiny proportion of the army in the civil war. Like never before, the Blacks fought in the Union army for their freedom with 186,097 black men in the Union army. Seven thousand one hundred and twenty-two officers and 178,975 enlisted soldiers and approximately Black sailors served in the Union Navy. If things had gotten even worse with senators dead or even Pelosi dead, I guarantee you that a civil war would have broken out in the USA once more, and this time it would have been far more deadly. The Blacks were preparing themselves whether this was organized or not, but for many, they were certain that a civil war was brewing as the Whites also were preparing for a race war. I am not surprised that it never happened, and it will never happen. You see, there is no need for another war. Some of you might have already guessed why.

They have already secured the physiological and technological infrastructure that will bound us to their will, so I never expected a civil war; still, the penalty will be one of their most significant outcomes for them at the end of their seven years or more terror. Already and we are at their beck and call. The few Black men who dare to challenge or question today's authority will feel a heavy blow. For many, they need not do anything as they hunt us down in their uniforms. They call themselves police men as they shoot us like dogs in the streets. Unlike the Black men of the Union Army, the men of today have had to retreat, some will be bold to fight back on their own in 2021, but this will be to their detriment and yet ending as the heroes like their counterparts of 1864.

You see, the paradox here is that the Whites are also retreating big time. For many, this is not noticeable, but, yes, they are fleeing with great fear because the war of 1864 is that of a completely different context, style and, narrative. Today, it is barely about black and white, not to take away the fact that the Blacks are still the central focus because they still are. However, the minds of this generation of Blacks, Whites and Asians have been so integrated with the advent of social media and technology that the 1% elites have included everyone in its new method of doing what they have always done, and these are to steal, kill and destroy.

The promise that Esau made to kill us, Jacob, just never stopped. They have even used false love to kill us in all the divisive ways you could never imagine. Executive orders will be signed with an appearance as if they are in our favour, but never be fooled. Their methods of deception and lies have gone to a different level that, for many like myself, we will never comprehend. They have had to make things far more inclusive, especially for the young Blacks so that when that great day of deception arrives, which by the way, I think is already here; those young ones who thought that finally, they have made it and that the glass ceiling has broken will come to realize that they have been cornered in a trap that they will not be able to get out of unless they choose death and inconceivable pain. These major pushbacks against the Black men will appear very inhumane but will be necessary for our own good and the desired outcome. With Covid 19, so much has been put in motion that has put us into lock downs, closing down the economies, increasing mental health illness amongst all, and worse of all, the increasing death of all; but with a major effect on the ethnic minorities; particularly the Black people. With these pushbacks, we have no power to stop them, and yet this is only the start with ten times worse to come, the birth pain in action. They are making sure that we are working behind the computer screens and by that way, they got us whenever, and however they want us.

For many, these pushbacks are real, some were only just about to see the light at the end of the tunnel with their future, and then these manufactured circumstances have kept us locked in with international significance. The closure of borders which have ultimately affected trade. Schools closed, fewer job opportunities, and for some complete loss of jobs have been just a few of the pushbacks but deliberate strategies to keep the people powerless and in order to have complete control over the people. Yet again, this was only the start as they will further impose on our personal space. Certainly, the virus exists, but that virus, for many, is very suspicious in its origin and sinister agenda. I am on board with those with such belief.

But alas; for how long? While all these scenarios have been taking place and everyone, including the White people and Asians, suddenly see their privileges being stripped away, the Black men are becoming more and more knowledgeable and united. Take a look at some YouTube channels such as Big Stone, also known as Claude Sinclair and also look at the YouTube channel of Kino, Good Life in Jamaica, and you will see changes that in most recent times appeared to be the impossible. It was as if suddenly and all the infighting and hate amongst our Blacks stopped instantaneously, everyone pooled in and supported each other. People from the UK, USA, Canada, Germany and sure, other places have entrusted Kino and have given Kino money to help those who have been oppressed and suppressed for so many years.

It is amazing, but not a surprise for me because the 400 years is up! Respect to M.P Phillip Paulwell who I saw being a part of Big Stone's initiative to ensure unity amongst infighting parties in the garrison communities.

My love for M.P Phillip Paulwell will always be there in my heart because he knows that he is one of us and his duty is to build. In any government that is rare because the government in my mind has always been part and parcel of the devil's servant and that is to steal, kill and destroy. You might think in your mind that I am being mindless here, but let us make a few points to justify such a statement. The hate in these communities did not happen overnight. They started as a seed planted by someone and groups outside of the garrison communities for sinister agendas. Before the seed was planted, the people were loving, law-abiding citizens. The guns did not walk into these precious citizen hands. So do not patronize us with your lessons as if you want to teach us how to love. We are love! The guns came from somewhere and it sure did not come from the land of Jamaica or from the hands of the people who are now able to rebuild their lives with love because Yah is now at the frontline so you can't touch us anymore... Your devilish policies, restrictions, and complete neglect came from the very people we entrusted the power over us, our own and their masters who through the IMF amongst other scams stole, killed and destroyed us. Over the years before and since independence you exploited them and then scorned them as if they were untouchables. I say this to my fellow Shemites. Be proud, you are coming from King David so stand straight and upright and tell your children that and let it ring in their ears forever. It was by design that you were made powerless to the evil that surrounded you. You did nothing wrong except that our fore fathers did not follow the laws of the Most High and ignored our Most High which caused us to be in this rot today. We can however say that the storm is almost over because our redemption draweth near as Yahua Yahushua Messhiach has already started to send the plagues to set his people free. He has started his wrath on those who have afflicted pain and death on us for 400 years. And, for all our Mothers, Fathers, Sons, daughters and Grandparents they have killed or caused suffering to, remember one thing. They can kill our bodies, but they can never kill our souls! Our people never died in vain and if you read the book of Enoch, then you will know that they are still alive right now enjoying the fountain of life and tranquillity ten times beyond this earth, while our adversaries are experiencing non-stop torment immediately upon their death. We did not need their dirty money then, and we do not need their money now. We will endure to the end.

Let me show you a few images of the man Kino and some of his foot soldiers that the Most High has been using to do some great work in getting back his people together as they were in the times of King David. I shall also mention some of the names of his donors who the Most High has also been using to get back his people together.

I fear no evil because we know that the Most High is the leader here, and no one, not one, whether it be physical, human, or spiritual forces, can stop what he has ordained.

Take a good look at our giants in Jamaica and those we have no image of in the USA, UK and elsewhere due to not getting their permission or not knowing their images; you are truly blessed souls who I pray Yah will continue to fill your baskets and keep you enriched and strong forever, in this world and the next. However, you must remember to keep his laws; otherwise it will not be blessings that will follow you but an eternal curse! I have the Ten Commandments above my bed so that I am always reminded of it, so I wish to remind you of the Ten Commandments.

Kino's team, One Team, Dream Team, Dream Team One Team. The foot soldiers, Yah's present day disciples!

Exodus 20

The Ten Commandments

And God spoke all these words:

[2] *"I am the LORD your God, who brought you out of Egypt, out of the land of slavery.*

[3] *"You shall have no other gods before[a] me.*

[4] *"You shall not make for yourself an image in the form of anything in heaven above or on the earth beneath or in the waters below.*

[5] *"You shall not bow down to them or worship them; for I, the LORD your God, am a jealous God, punishing the children for the sin of the parents to the third and fourth generation of those who hate me,*

[6] *but showing love to a thousand generations of those who love me and keep my commandments.*

[7] *"You shall not misuse the name of the LORD your God, for the LORD will not hold anyone guiltless who misuses his name.*

[8] *"Remember the Sabbath day by keeping it holy.*

[9] *Six days you shall labor and do all your work,*

[10] *but the seventh day is a sabbath to the LORD your God. On it you shall not do any work, neither you, nor your son or daughter, nor your male or female servant, nor your animals, nor any foreigner residing in your towns.*

¹¹ For in six days the LORD made the heavens and the earth, the sea, and all that is in them, but he rested on the seventh day. Therefore, the LORD blessed the Sabbath day and made it holy.

¹² "Honour your father and your mother, so that you may live long in the land the LORD your God is giving you.

¹³ "You shall not murder.

¹⁴ "You shall not commit adultery.

¹⁵ "You shall not steal.

¹⁶ "You shall not give false testimony against your neighbour.

¹⁷ "You shall not covet your neighbour's house. You shall not covet your neighbour's wife, or his male or

female servant, his ox or donkey, or anything that belongs to your neighbour. "

Their theme is very catchy but extremely effective; One team, dream team, Dream team, one team, and this theme is solid with love and unity. They help the sick, the hungry, the homeless, and their message is always inspiring. Their donors are passionate about helping their fellowmen as they entrust their donations to Kino, who never fail the donors or the people. What we will have next is Kino teaching other communities in Jamaica to do the same because this is Yah's way, and we get stronger and stronger every day. They must unite and get stronger because what is coming their way; our way will be the fight of their lives like no man has ever seen on this planet since it has been created by the Most High. It will be the tribulation, and it will get stronger as the enemy realizes more and more that they are losing their grip of power. The enemy has already started with the virus, vaccination, and the last stage to force everyone to be chipped.

And unfortunately, many of them will fall unless they keep strong and united and never take the mark of the beast which is here!

Revelation 13: 16-18

[16]And he causeth all, both small and great, rich and poor, free and bond, to receive a mark in their right hand, or in their foreheads: [17]And that no man might buy or sell, save he that had the mark, or the name of the beast, or the number of his name.

[18]Here is wisdom. Let him that hath understanding count the number of the beast: for it is the number of a man, and his number is Six hundred threescore and six.

It will be a tough one because this is about our generation. This prophecy is no longer some distance information that we use to scoff at because it was not tangible then. It is very tangible now.

I must highlight and 'big up' some of the donors from Kino's team, One Team, Dream Team.

First of all, the Dream Team is for me, the greatest because what they are doing for the community is more than any donations that they can receive because they are donors themselves as they donate their services to those who need it the most in the community. Saying that other donors are most appreciated, so we thank;

Keisha and family from the USA, Unknown from Canada, The Overcomers from the USA, Ricardo from the USA, Ms. Nana from the UK, Eric from New York USA, Lisa from the UK, Country girl from the UK, Catherines from the UK, Ray from Germany, Jay Bell from Canada, Lady Dee from the UK, Warren AKA Bounty from the UK, Three friends from Greenwich Wood Nursing Home New York, Sophia and Courtney from the USA, Devon and Tony from Brooklyn New York. If I have left anyone out, please forgive me, but you are surely in the Most High thoughts, and that for me is more important.

Let the record be set straight though. We the Shemites, Israelites never will accept anything that is not good for our body. No form of drugs is ever welcome because we have had enough of the negatives being supplied to our people. We do not want any more of that, and our leader Yahuah Yahushua Messhiach will not allow it anymore! We have had negatives such as the corrupt music and drugs from other sources, and we will not have it anymore. The 400 years is up!

We have no choice but to be united because soon, when the full force is meted out against us, we will have no one but ourselves and if you are not sure if this is true, well just give it a few months, a year, or two, and if luck is with us, then we might be able to enjoy a year before the terror strikes. And for those who might not have already noticed, the terror has already begun with the fear of covid 19 and the force of the vaccinations. Whoever control your minds controls you, and that is always the ultimate aim; just remember that.

Kino's team, One Team, Dream Team, Dream Team One Team. The foot soldiers, Yah's present day disciples!

We also have AKA, Big Stone but his true name is Claude Sinclair and his help amongst our community is just as rewarding because the Most High is behind him 100 percent. He knows how passionate I am about his work in our community and with this book I hope that he will continuously be raised up, and frankly he does not need me to raise him up because this has been doing of the Most High Yahua Yahushua Messhiach, and no one can stop this. Here are some images of Big Stone with some of his great work.

This is Claude Sinclair, and he is very active in helping the entertainers who have been used and abused and in the same breath, he has been equally active in helping in the community with those who are needy regarding food, clothing and shelter, but what struck a chord for me was how he, Little Lenny and Ritchie Stevens helped the angel who was in our midst. Her name was Yvonne Sterling. The story was how she was robbed by her producers and for years lived in the most forbidden conditions with water surrounding her inside and outside of her house. Mr Sinclair being a record producer of the label Big Stone

Records allowed him to get the help of Little Lenny and Ritchie Stevens and the rest was history.

Here is Mr Claude Sinclair with Yvonne Sterling, the angel whom he was instrumental in helping her back on her feet.

She was able to rebuild her life, and she released a song with and with the help of Ritchie Stevens and Little Lenny; thank you, Lord, For What you've done for me. An amazing song. Not long after, she sadly passed away, but she was taken by the Most High as he had proven her righteousness, and she was to demonstrate to us that it was never about her or us but the Most High.

This movement will only get stronger amongst our people as we learn more and more that we are from Kings and Queens and that Yahua Yahusha Messhiach is and forever our leader.

Claude Sinclair never advertised what he has done for people such as Kadeen with lupus, Arianna whom he helped back to school, and many more. His passion for the welfare of his country and his people is undeniable. We know our friends from our enemies, and it is time to embrace our friends and get rid of the enemies, and don't you worry, we will smoke them out because the enemy's time is up. It has been 400 years now, so those who have been killing our daughters, sons, mothers, father, and grandparents, your time is up! Even if you are a Shemite like us, we will weed you out in due course. We are watching you, and we know who you are!

We are already seeing the terror with job loss and the constant terror from the police all over the world, but worse in the USA. Suddenly and your sons and daughters are being shot in the streets like dogs.

What more evidence do you need? Through social media such as youtube and the news we are seeing examples such as a White policeman telling a White female who held her hands in the air with great fear, only to be pacified by the Police telling her that she need not be fearful because she is White and that the Police only kill Blacks. Sound callous of the Police man, but he was telling the truth. What more evidence can you ask for when on every platform you can see a Black man with no weapon being shot to death as he runs with his back to the policeman? Might I add that the same happens in Black countries such as Jamaica because it is the same Babylon system. They are following the same script!

What more evidence can you ask for? An innocent harmless child at the age of 17 being shot dead in Sanford, Florida on 26th February 2012 and his murderer George Michael Zimmerman was acquitted on July 13th 2013.

In the next world, I can tell you that he shall never be acquitted because his ass will be on fire eternally. He will not be able to return to tell us, but I can tell you from now that it is a promise made from Yah. So, George, enjoy all that you got now in this short life span on earth. Your time is coming!

The hate builds up amongst everyone as injustice continues year in year out, and so it is no surprise that Black Lives Matter has become a house hold name amongst the people, and at the same time, the increase in the right-wings increases daily until they have come out of their caves to show themselves up at the steps of Capitol Hill.

Believe me when I say that the hate is real and it has always been like that, but an incident reminds me of just how different the Black people can be, although it is never the definitive persona of Black people, as you will soon learn later in my writing of this book.

How many of you saw where the White police had handcuffed a Black man and while the Black man was handcuffed, White brother started to choke on a chewing gum that he swallowed. The police was choking to death and was even on the ground trying to get rid of that chewing gum. The Black man looked on and appeared as if he was pondering to run, but in the split of a second told his White brother by blood.

I will keep reminding you that we are brothers by blood because most of us did not realize that by Rebecca and Isaac, we came from the same parents;

the same womb of Rebecca. Anyway, to get back to the incident, his Black brother told him to give him the key to release himself and save him. The White police relented and gave up the key.

Many must have held their breath at that moment and thought that the Black man would have run off. Oh no, instead, the Black brother lifted his White brother, stood behind him, and supported his chest from behind with his hand pumping his chest. He had the police leaned forward so that the chewing gum blocking his airway would come out of his mouth. He gave about five or six sharp blows to the back and chest, and then you could see the gum flying out of the mouth of the policeman. He saved that policeman's life.

The handcuff was on the ground still, and then, to my surprise, the Black man went for the handcuff and gave it to the Police to handcuff him again. I expected the police to handcuff him just the same, but to my surprise, the policeman told him to go because he saved his life. I choked back tears because very seldom you see the heart being softened like that and that only showed that not everyone is like that.

Although he only responded like that because good came to him at that moment, there are many great stories of White people showing love and care for his Black brother but the hate will get worse, and all race will show serious discontent and hate as the birth pain increases. This is a proof that things don't have to be the way it is, but the oppression has to be the same because this is how Esau has rolled even before he came from Rebecca's womb.

As that experience of the policeman saved by that Black man came to my mind, the number of Blacks in prison just came to mind, most of whom I am certain are innocent, framed or incarcerated for the most absurd reasons due to hate and evil perpetrated against the Black man. One that many people are totally unaware of is that ever since the black man had the right to vote. The prison was strategically used to prevent the Black man to vote, paving the way for the rights of the White supremacist to lead without any challenge to their policy of hate. Even a simple human right such as the right to vote was a struggle for the Black man since the 1800s with William Garner who was refused the rights to vote in the State of Kentucky.

He was not the last to be slaughtered for his simple act of voting, as in the 1920s, scores of Blacks were slaughtered for that very reason. The fear to the back of their heads must have been, what next? They will want to be the President of the United States of America, so incarcerating young Black men to this very day has been their primary strategy at play. Let us face it; incarceration is no different from slavery and breaking the spirit of any human being. About 2.3 million people make up the total population in the USA's prison alone, with Black Americans incarcerated five times more than White people.

In some States, that statistics doubled to 10% for the Black men incarcerated. Oklahoma, with 2,625 Black prisoners per 100,000 residents, and yet, Oklahoma only has 7.7% Black people living there. No other state is worse than that, but the rest are not far from Oklahoma's statistics. May I remind you that Rebecca was told that there were two great nations fighting in her womb, this is only part of the outcome of the war that Rebecca was told. You see, the White man knows that it is between him and us, and so they will do everything to keep us down in ensuring that their rule never ends. They have been playing dirty before they got out of Rebecca's womb, but the Caucasians know that their time is up now, so they will not get dirty now, but very muddy. They have all the documents in the Vatican and other places because it was them who raided us and took everything from us since 70 AD.

They have even made the prison into a business where they can profiteer from us being in prisons. Do not get me wrong; they are not playing the Black people alone because when you look at it from a different context; the USA is the home of 5% of the world's population, and yet it makes up a quarter of the world's prisoners. Certainly, you can see that the few in power have made these souls, irrespective of their race, into slaves. The USA is nothing but a mass slave camp.

They make billions from incarceration, but more so, from the Black youths targeted by private prison companies who have been making huge profits, to say the least, out of these people being in prisons. According to the American Civil liberties Union; in 2010, the two largest prison companies, Corrections

Corporation of America and The GEO Group Inc. alone, received \$3 billion in revenues. Their top executives each received annual compensation packages worth more than 3 million dollars. Lobbying plays a vital role in these private prison companies, with more than 45 million dollars per year lobbying state and federal governments, further spending on election campaigns of governors, state legislators, and judges. How much worse can this get. And so nothing has changed. It is no wonder that people, irrespective of their race, are angry and seek to blame someone.

They all have a right to be angry because putting aside the evidence of incarceration, you only need to go into the 'free' public to see that we, the 'free' ones are very much incarcerated in the same way. Any morning from 6 am onwards, and as you travel through the metropolitan of New York, London, and other major cities, the guards are at the barriers, and there are so many barriers that you might as well call them prison gates.

The guards are always there in a militant way to see your tickets. If that does not make you a prisoner, then the unbearable labour, expensive housing, limited space in the homes, bills tied around your necks, and I could go on are enough to make you a prisoner indeed. Some people would rather to be in their gated prison than their opened prison called 'freedom.'

The problem here is that Esau's children control the media; both the print, electronic and social media, and so they have been force feeding the public at large with the hate against immigrants and Blacks from day one to the point where even the immigrants are believing it and fighting against themselves. Therefore, lies prevail again, and their Black brothers again are in the firing line. With them being able to turn on and off the hate rhetoric or narratives as they please, they can amass the right-wings to their wings and hence the results of a led mass Capitol Insurrection.

Come on now, never lose track of the theme here. The Caucasian's 400 years is up, and they know it! The transition of power from Esau to Jacob's children has begun, and this time when the birth pain has fully taken place in the next seven or more years, it will be the Most High who will be leading with Jacob's children being his servants. So no longer will they be able to bring any harm to Jacob's children.

It must come with sacrifices at first, though, with the increase in hatred, more blood spill, hating your parents, family and giving them up to the enemy, hunger and starvation and no jobs will all be the outcome for many, but for few death will be the ultimate sacrifice and the only alternative if you are to be in favour of The Most High, still it will be worth it as redemption draws nearer.

That redemption can never come from any other one but Yahuah Yahushua Messhiach.

Anyone who attempts to save the children of Jacob, though honourable it may seem; except for the Most High will be put down and unless Yah allows it for his own purpose as I believe he had done with Moses and Harriet Tubman, then expect the worse. All these men were put down, some in more vicious ways than others, but they all had one thing in common and that was attempting to do what Yah had already done, and will finish up, and that was to save the children of Jacob. No one can save the children of Jacob. Not Marcus Garvey, Not Fred Hampton from the Black

Panther, Not John F Kennedy, Not Martin Luther King, Not Haile Selassie, or any other but Yahua Yahushua Messhiach. Some have called his name Jesus Christ; some believe that he is White, but all due to ignorance, their sub-conscious minds remain in a state of confusion to their detriment, I say. Never the less this need not be a debate since it is of little relevance when you follow the scripture that says that you should worship the Creator in spirit and in truth, and there is no other desire that he asked of you.

So far, we have seen how the Whites have subjected us Shemites to unbearable oppression through the lenses of hatred, but who said that it has only been the Whites alone or as many would like us to believe that they were the only ones who have subjected us to hate and oppression. Not through my lens because this is where many of you will be disappointed with me as I eventually tear the layers off to reveal that in some cases, the Whiteman are merely used as cover for the true and mast vile hate that has been shown against us. For many, it will be a surprise to learn that that hate is closer to home than you think.

Let us leave that for a later chapter, though, as I further link my thoughts to the Capitol Insurrection.

Was the insurrection staged? You make up your mind. Esau is like a drowning man holding onto the straw, and so at this stage, he will drown anyone with him. All I know is that the hate is real, and they are determined to keep that control and have complete control by any means necessary. They are determined that no one, not even their own, will get in their way. They are therefore using technology to its fullest, and now race is the least of their issue, but it is everything.

However, their largest obstacle is the Black people, particularly the Shemites. Whether you are Black, White, or Asian, we are all now vulnerable. Confusing though it may seem, the narrative has changed somewhat because the enemy has integrated all race to fight with him because he must try to prevent the main leader of the Shemites and those who have genuinely converted from returning, and the Caucasian in control knows that he cannot do so, so Esau's children foolishly delude themselves that they can stall The Most High's return.

Everyone has become a possible victim because Esau is determined to bring down everyone with his eyes set on the prize; the true Hebrew Israelites or the Shemites. We will be the most stubborn to do as he says, so they will suffer the most.

The hate has reached a depth that is beyond all imaginations, so when we hear people having their suspicions and fears, do not readily call it a conspiracy because these evil doers have the only intentions to steal, kill and destroy so do not put anything past them. When you hear the word conspiracy, just see it as a dim word that they coined for their sinister deceptions.

Despite people seeing what was once described as a conspiracy to be unfolding swiftly as reality in front of their eyes, many are still calling it conspiracy as they are being taken further into the abyss. Here I give you some of the suspicions; you can take it or leave it, but never dismiss it because it affects us whether you are Black, White, or Asian. Some have said that the testings for Covid 19 has been about the collection of our DNA's while some are a lot more elaborate and detailed have this to say; like this one, I am about to

111

share with you. Some even say that the vaccine has nano-technology in it, and you cannot blame them for having no trust in the government who have never been for the people and who live, breed, and feed us on everlasting lies from the dawn of day.

The fear-mongering from covid-19 linked to the threat of a closed down economy and to the back of the peoples' minds, the fear of death have led them to do just about everything, including everything to the whims and fancies of the government. I am sure that many never saw their country being a part of one world dictatorship, but they live in it and adhering to it at the same time. Who would not when the media runs the propaganda every day with anchor men such as Lester Holt drilling the messages of Covid 19 with the narratives of different strains and the deadly effects of unimaginable deaths that we only see on the news. Many have their suspicions that the death toll is all lies, with some asking where are the over burden funeral homes or funerals. Yes, they believe that the deaths exist, but some say that many doctors have been paid to put false information of Covid being the cause of death on an individual's death certificates. I am not sure what to believe, but knowing the desperation of Esau, I shall put nothing past them. Absolutely nothing!

Many believe that the man of perdition is here on earth this minute, and I am inclined to agree with them 100%. Some said that it was Obama, while others believed that it was Donald Trump. I do not know.

What I do know is that something is not right because the Covid 19 is systematically leading us towards a sinister structured path, even though we even hear that there is a cure for it.

Never forget that whether this is a talk from the peoples' mouths or not, this same talk came from Donald Trump himself. Donald Trump described Dr Stella Immanuel, who was born in Cameroon and is based in the Texan City of Houston as "very impressive". He was referring to the drug hydroxychloroquine that she claimed had cured patients with Covid-19.

"Nobody needs to get sick. This virus has a cure - it is called hydroxychloroquine; I have treated over 350 patients and not had one death."

Dr. Immanuel said. Donald Trump and his son retweeted her statements. Now when you see a President who is made to be racist sides with a Black doctor like this, I think that we all should have paid attention, and we did. We spent so much attention that Facebook and Twitter took down his and her viral messages and videos, saying that it violated their policies about misinformation. This dilemma is where we are today as the new world order muscles in its lack of freedom of speech and nondemocratic characteristics.

We are all in it, and therefore, it does not matter if you are Black, White, or Asian, the conspiracy rhetoric to throw you off from researching where technology is really at today is real, and its hate sits at the heart of its success. We are now in the era of nano dust, nano particles, smart dust, and the fusing of technology and human biology, known as synthetic biology.

You, therefore, must be aware and be alert to other information that you hear like this one:

'Artificial intelligence, human gene editing and advance robotic are all characteristics of this fusion of technology that blurs the line between the physical, digital and biological worlds.' This quote came from the Gov.UK website.

This quote makes sense when Hitachi makes a nano chip that is only 1/7th of 1 millimetre squared inside. It has a GPS capability called smart dust since it can be sprayed on us, absorbed in the sweat pores of the skin, taken in foods, drinks, injected, and also inserted through the nasal passages with a cotton swab. Are your alarm bells ringing yet? Let me know when it does.

Esau has become so desperate to holding onto his power and not wanting to transfer that power that he has no power to stop, so this is how low he has resorted to, and millions have already been subjected to this technology by indirect force.

They have a two-access magnetic sensor to track direction, an accelerator metre to track speed, light intensity sensor and temperature sensor and also transmit wireless to the smart grid internet and the cloud. This is literally hooked up to its human biological host to the smart grid tracking system like a walking breathing smartphone.

John Hopkins University received 870 million dollars from the Gates Foundation and has developed a version of smart dust called the GRIPPER. It is alleged that there are dozens of these on the swabs, the very swabs that you are being told to push up your nose to test if you got Covid 19; and I completely believe this to be true because Esau's children are determined to keep that power and prevent the transition of power that is imminent.

This was inspired by a parasitic worm that digs its teeth into the host's intestine or blood-brain area and can latch onto an intestinal mucosa and can release drugs, poison, or smart dust into the human body

My nose has always been to smell, the exit point for my body to excrete poison through mucus in a safe way. Not for someone to push some object up there every week as is being done in some places. The use of nano carriers provides a way for the nasal delivery of antigenic molecules, meaning a fast way to poison your interstitial fluids up your nose.

For many like myself, this is unbelievable and is therefore easily dismissed as a conspiracy, but remember one thing.

The biggest lie that most people have bought into and that is satan does not exist. Not because you cannot see him, he does not exist, but when you finally realize your deception, you will wish you believed from day one, but a little too late it shall be.

Seriously though, it begs the question, are we being tested, or vaccinated or nano chipped without our consent, or through deceptive means. If so, why, what could be the sinister reasons. Some say that it is to control our minds to further their evil agenda. Perhaps to set in place an easier ability to control our minds for the ultimate agenda to chip us all as some have called it, the mark of the beast.

The few who have gone on the streets to protest have been closed down by laws and legislations all backed up by the risks of this Covid 19. It seems to me as if they have had us by the balls, but let us continue.

What is at the end of the covid swab for the covid test? Are they putting nano particles into our brains through the nasal passage in order to manipulate our minds with these sinister technologies? They are at the last phase of their wicked work, and soon, we truly will see a different world. Different people which we already see anyway.

Morgellons fibres are allegedly on the tip of these covid swabs. On the tip of the covid swab, someone said that he found TC- Technetium (element 43), a radioactive transition metal with bio infiltrator properties such as mind control and DNA direct manipulation holographic optical chip and this was found at the end of the same swab.

Another image was shown of the threads of the swab moving and how they were very much alive.

If we are to believe that all of this is true, then we will be dismissed as loopy and mad, but if you deny the possibilities of this being true, then you are entirely crazy, just as it was said that a covid passport is all conspiracy and mad talk, but look! It is very much in full practice in Israel now and is being considered in most countries.

If that is not madness, then what is? All of these actions are out of hate but even more so; out of the desperation to hold onto complete control, and we are all now at a stage of we will either sink or swim and I am afraid that for the most; it will be sink as they are already sinking.

Chapter 8

President Obama and President Joe Biden

I t sounds like a paradox, but my favourite president of all time is President John F Kennedy. I know that I have said that he was put down for trying to save our people and exposing the dark world and he was put down, but, never the less he and the other heroes had a place, and it had to be known that it was never their place to save the children of Jacob. Their work, I believe, is nevertheless, deeply appreciated.

Why? Well, he was the only president that I know of, who had called the agents of the devil out for what they indeed are at the Waldorf – Astoria Hotel, New York City, on April 27, 1961. At this speech to the American Newspaper Publishers Association. In this speech, he defends the right to freedom of speech but went further and dared to speak against the secret societies. He must have been a marked man from then, and indeed, by November 22, 1963, he was brutally murdered. He was a man of virtue who fought for the rights of not only the poor but also the Black man. During this time, we had Black men at their fullest fighting for equality with the greats like Martin Luther King Jr; the Civil Rights leader was murdered at Lorraine Motel in Memphis, Tennessee on April 4, 1968, and Malcolm X another giant who fought for the rights of Black men murdered on February 21, 1965. It was not by coincidence that these men felt empowered to speak and act the way they did. It was also no coincidence that all three men were brutally murdered in the same way within the same era. All men murdered two to three years apart of each men. Surely not by coincidence.

The point stands that while I only recognize Yahuah Yahsua Messhiach as the only saviour of all people, I must admit that these men had put their lives at risk and paid dearly. No other President can be acknowledged as being selfless as President John F Kennedy was. Many are quick to highlight Abraham Lincoln, but I will be equally quick to alert you to the fact that Abraham Lincoln fervently disagreed with Blacks having any public positions mixing with Whites or ever voting. This, I will say, came from his mouth. He never owned a slave, but I can see why that mud has stuck on him even to this day.

Former President Obama and current President Joe Biden can never walk in the same boot as President John F Kennedy. Now more than ever, we need someone like President John F Kennedy, Martin Luther King, Fred Hampton from the Black Panther, and Malcolm X to fight and be willing to die for us, but not even one leader around the world has the guts to stand up to the secret society who are murdering us in open sight. For those without the goggles on, you would have seen that our greatest threat is the government which was meant to protect and serve us. However, they are rooted in deception, lies, and murder.

They continue to do what their master does, and these are to steal, kill and destroy. I will wait for all the prophecies to be fulfilled to prove who the anti-Christ is. I pray never to be fooled. They are all cowards. It does not matter where in the world you are, the Church and the governments have teamed up together, and they have become our greatest disappointment. The stage has always been perfectly set with each and every one assigned tasks that have led to the present outcome of events worldwide. The Pope has already set in place for the One World Religion and the government is, by the looks of things, soon give its powers to the Pope. It is only a matter of time now.

The New World Order is set, and a crucial point I would like to make here is that each and every one of these leaders; Presidents, have had their roles to play. Their roles were well set before they were elected or inaugurated. Let us quickly look at some examples.

The 1991 Persian Gulf War, also known as Operation Desert Storm, was in President George Bush Snr time when he declared.

"More than one small country; it is a big idea; a New World Order" with "new way of working"

So all those who thought that it was about the oil, weapons of mass destruction, and all other thoughts, you can rest all of them to bed because George Bush

Snr made is clear from day one what it was all about, the New World Order.

They knew that George Bush Snr was fitted for all of that evil, so he was elected whether the people wanted him or not. This New World Order was what George Bush Snr mandate of Presidency was all about.

Then there was President Bill Clinton; Bill Clinton was perfect for his role of getting even more Blacks in prison. Bill Clinton was 'elected' in January 20, 1993 and at that time the population of Black inmates in Federal and State prisons was about 1,290,000, while there were 109,000 Black females incarcerated. By the end of Bill Clinton serving Presidency of January 20, 2001 there were 2,166,000 Black males incarcerated, while there were 231,000 Black females incarcerated in the USA. These statistics came from the Bureau of Justice Statistics.

This massive difference in numbers was an outcome of Bill Clinton 1994 Crime bill which was authored and supported by no other but Joseph Biden. All enemies of the Black race. Joe Biden was the Chairman of the 1994 Crime Bill.

Joe Biden was the one responsible for putting in mandatory sentencing. It is further alleged that Bill Clinton took donations from private prisons in return for tougher laws to fill up the prisons. The thing here is that all these outcomes did not come by chance. They came with deliberate intentions, and which was to kill, destroy and steal from the Black people.

Bill Clinton's actions of the free trade treaties were the pre-requisites to the high crimes that engulfed the black communities, destroying any chance they had at getting a job, and in return, the crime bill gave them the prison cells. So Bill did well for his master; he did what he was mandated. And then there was George W Bush Junior. He was elected on the 20th January 2001 and served his terms to the 20th January 2009.

He was truly fit for purpose. He was their perfect man for the Iraq invasion. The deception of the weapon of mass destruction with his crony Tony Blair was a successful narrative only to be proven to be all lies. Please note that the likes of Condoleezza Rice, a Black woman was very much at the helm of 2003 invasion of Iraq.

She was the National Security Advisor, she endorsed and instructed for waterboarding to take place, and, I could go on because all that has been said is enough to describe her as an ogre and evil soul who has danced with the devil and has blood on her hands. Another Black Shemite involved in the depth of this evil was Colin Powell who has Jamaican heritage, but boy he got blood on his hands. On the 5th February 2003 he delivered a presentation to make a case for the war with Iraq at the United Nations. He was the Secretary Of State under the regime of no other but former President George Bush Sr.

Let us be clear on all of this, the declaration of his George Bush Senior in 1991 remained the same in 2003, and that was with the narrative.

"More than one small country; it is a big idea; a New World Order" with "new way of working".

That new way of working is called the reset, the age of reset which we are currently at. This is why we are all locked up in our homes, losing our jobs, and moving towards a cashless society.

That is why the Capitol Insurrection was done with perfect calculation to distract us so that they can continue with their sinister agenda. With people's opinion on Condoleeza Rice, Colin Powell, many other Black men, many believe that Esau has now integrated a few of his blood Brother Jacob to help him do the job of doing the complete destruction of his hated brother Jacob.

So Jacob is being used to destroy Jacob, and still it shall not work out for them. It will only prove that no matter what you throw at the Most High you can never defeat him. Never!

This is why such a battle can never be won with Jacob alone, and that is why the true leader of Jacob's children Yahua Yahushua Messhiach will need to step in and fight the battle for us, making us victorious once and for all. The struggle goes on as the true aim is to steal, kill, and destroy.

During George Bush Jr, it was clear that with so much going on, the scales of the people worldwide were starting to fall off. People were waking up at a very slow rate, but still, they were waking up, and they predicted that this would have happened, and so something had to happen, must happen. All nations started to question the agenda since the Twin Towers collapsed on the 11th September 2001, and with later events, such as the Iraq invasion, the questions and suspicions became further intense. They did not know what to believe anymore. They were seeing their future and their children falling apart, and this was indeed an international cause for concern for the common man. Most were still not awoken as some speculated that the invasion was all about the oil. Some were thinking heck, I might be their next target, not realizing that they were already the target.

Although, saying that, I remember clearly how people from all over the world were rejoicing exceedingly from the collapse of the Twin Towers, one of the indications that they saw the West as actual enemies. The West was also thinking differently from the day that you had the collapse of the Twin Towers; they were already attacking their citizens, and so when the Capitol Insurrection occurred, it was another direct message that it was no longer of foreign countries, but as Nancy Pelosi called it; 'domestic terrorist attack'; even requesting a 9/11 style commission to investigate the Capitol riots. Too little too late, though. We know what is happening; we are just waiting to see what is next. Only A matter of time before when you finally decide to realize the truth, only to find that you are now one of the persecuted ones. Too little too late.

With that said. The puppeteers realized that it was time to take out the next trick from the box, and out came President Barack Obama. What perfect timing, although this was all planned decades ago. What ideal man to have taken over from George W Bush Jr. George Bush played the clown, but he did exactly as he was told. He bombed, he slaughtered, he destroyed while he played the clown, the fool, the gimmicks; hell I had my chuckle at his stupid comments and awkward or even embarrassing moments, but all that gimmick was over since in the end, he really played us the fools with 800,000-1,3 million deaths, 4.5 million displaced Iraqis,1.2 million widows, 5 million orphans and thousands in the USA and British force lost their lives.

We were played as he entertained us playing the buffoon while he and Blair butchered the Iraqis, including Sadam Hussein and members of the armed force under lies of weapons of mass destruction, only to get to the reset where we are today. he was no fool, correction; his masters were no fool, they knew very fully well what they were doing.

While we were laughing and criticizing him, he was killing like a raging mad man. Their tactics never change, distract while we steal, kill and destroy. In the end, it was no laughing matter as he and the rest of the enemies got us where they wanted us.

George Bush Jr was now replaced with someone articulate, of class, extremely bright, a professional lawyer, and so, here was the big prize for the world. Wait for it.

He was a Black man. This new President of the United States of America had made world history. The first Black man to have become the President of The United States Of America. The most powerful country in the world. This was unheard of. Nothing is new under the sun because this tactic of distraction was not new, and it had happened just when people were starting to become suspicious of events that were speeding up. Many will now be disgusted that I have said that Barack Obama's rise to power was by a sinister design and worse to distract the people of the world.

Come on now, how many people heard of him before, and did he not rise to power when the world was highly furious at the West destroying the most vulnerable nations of the world. What was the reaction of the people when Barack Obama was elected? It was of elation like we have never seen before. The celebrations in the streets, the responses from Blacks, Whites, and Asians were of exceeding numbers. Almost all seemed to be rejoicing, except for Donald Trump, of course.

The one thing that I can never take from Obama, and that is, of all the USA leaders, or of all the 46 Presidents, Barack Obama, in my opinion has been the most charismatic and again, in my opinion, the most intelligent of them all. He knew exactly how to make the people accept that he was the best. Can you remember the hook line and sinker 'Yes I Can,' which Obama caught us with? He has, however, been the one that I have been most suspicious of because he has a unique hold on most people all over the world, and that is irrespective of their race, culture, and religion. Many believe that he has never left the Presidency, many are still yearning for him to return as they compared him to Donald Trump, and that is fair when you look at the chaos that Trump has brought with the Presidency.

His charms and charisma have won over many Blacks, Whites, Latinos, and Asians.

This is undoubtedly something to celebrate, and I am certain that many Blacks would skin me should I utter any negative thoughts about him. However, I shall, and I would expect for you to compare me to Candace Owen, in fact I was compared to Candace Owen and Shaun Bailey on Facebook. Outrageous! I am an unknown individual so the comparison should have been thrown out this instance. There are however, many things that Candace has said of which I am in agreement with, but clearly, my opinion as well as many other people, Black people mainly who believes that she is on the enemy's side and I doubt that she will return to her own, if ever she was there in the first place. She must answer to the Most High, so that is between her and the Most High.

I had to rebuke that individual firmly and made it be known that under no circumstances am I of their kind. I love my Black people, but no more than I love

Yah, Yahua Yahushua Messhiach, and the Holy Spirit.

Subsequently, I am obliged to say it as it is because it is only a matter of time that Black people, White, and Asians will be led to the abattoir, and at that moment, they will not be able to say give me another chance, As much as I focus on Black people, we are all in it, but for the Black people, they will be singled out because of who they are, and they need to be aware of this. Let us get back to former President Barack Obama. You see, former President Barack Obama did a lot that some would say was good. The best, in my opinion, was the Obama care. He got the Health care reform in place, ensuring Patient protection and Affordable Care Act. He also had the clean power plan as he addressed Climate change.

There was also Race to the Top competitive grant programme for education, and then we had the Lilly Ledbetter fair pay act, One of his biggest legacy has been the forwarding of the LGBTQ communities, especially amongst the Black communities, and these were only a few of his achievements.

I can think of more than 20 more. However, many Black people have said that he has done little to nothing for them with regards to employment, crime, and so on, and I get it that the Republicans vetoed many of the policies that he was determined to introduce for the betterment of not just Black people, but everyone.

My issue has never been about his achievements or his race. My issue as it should have been with any of the government leaders, is the agenda that has been underway to control us and that they all are playing a part in this insidious governance. I for one, do not believe that former President Obama is excluded from this plot; if anything, I believe that he is at the centre of it all. I trust none of them. Until they can speak and defend the people like former President John F Kennedy had done.

So former President Obama played his part and role perfectly as mandated, but do I think we have seen the end of him. I doubt it, pretty much. He is a lot more than what I believe we think he is. The plot thickens, though, as we get to Former President Donald Trump.

With Donald Trump, I was most confused because he played his part so well, I was never sure just which side he was on.

He played the part of a thorough bred racist well, and at the same time he was very appealing to many Blacks. To the point where many black people were leaving the Democratic Party to the Republican Party. He had a role, and he was outstanding in his role. You can never deny that he, too, was mandated and was fixed like the rest of them. He was certainly the most controversial and chaotic President that the world has ever seen. His successor, Joseph Biden described him as the worst President of them all. I shall not dwell on him for too long, but I shall say this much, his predecessor appeared to work very hard to have him lost to Hilary Clinton. Michelle Obama with her speech:

'When they go low, we go high.' This statement alone could have given Hilary the crown to break that glass ceiling that she appeared to be desperate to achieve. In my mind, this was all a load of BS. The scandal on Hilary was all timed to ensure that she never broke that ceiling. I would not be surprised if she knew exactly what was going on. They are all actors, and they are all in the act.

It is in my humble opinion that Donald Trump was all set for the Presidency decades ago, and he was the perfect fit due to the circumstances.

Out of chaos, they control, and there was no better man of chaos than former President Donald Trump. Hilary Clinton could never have caused not even a fraction of the chaos that Donald Trump was employed to wreak. He was commissioned to wreak havoc, and he certainly did. This election result had nothing to do with Hilary being a female before I am bashed as a sexist, but due to the fact as earlier described that Donald Trump had earned the reputation as a hater, racist, and the man of chaos.

He was often described as a narcissist and a rebellious brat with the need for a dummy in his mouth so that he can be made quiet and even that would not have pacified him. They needed total chaos in the world to fully launch the reset. This reset was the greatest mammoth of job for them with the offset of Covid 19, Lock down, and so on. The New World Order government was at its last stage of getting the reset in place, and Donald Trump was their man to distract and deflect the people even with their lockdown throughout the world.

He ended his legacy with a bang to let the World know his fitness for purpose, and this was the Capitol Insurrection.

His speech stirred the emotions of his supporters, telling them that he will be there with them at Capitol Hill. Of Course, he was never to be with them as they caused complete anarchy.

I say anarchy with no apology because Donald Trump was the President, and yet he was leading this uprising. This was not leadership, especially when at the save America Rally in Washington, he said:

"Sop the steal." of the election as he wanted them to go to the Capitol to demonstrate against Congress certifying President-elect Joe Biden's victory.

The supporters in return gallantly shouting; "Fight for Trump! Fight for Trump! Fight for Trump."

What happened next was just savage, and yet nothing came out of it. Of course, nothing would have come out of that because in my opinion it was all scripted even before he was elected, my mistake, selected as the President of the United States of America.

Well, here are the give-aways. The authorities, such as the US Capitol Police were completely aware of the threat of violence three days before the pro-Trump insurgents overwhelmed USCP officers. Heck, the police had let them in as if they were welcoming a crash party.

The USCP memo also warned that there would be white supremacist amid militia members' gate crashers on the 6th of January at the Capitol Hill. This information was given three days before and yet there was nothing done to try to stop this.

Had it been the Black Lives Matter protest, the number of Black bodies lining the streets would be uncountable, and they would not have even gotten two hundred yards to the entrance or gate of Capitol Hill. Well, just look at the amount of security that filled the streets just a year before the Capitol Insurrection when the BLM protested. I somehow believe that narrative would never have played out because then the script would have been read wrong.

Windows were smashed in, offices were looted and destroyed, 4 rioters dead and a policeman dead, and still nothing happened to President Donald Trump. He was acquitted!!

Sacrilege of the Speaker of the House's Office, Nancy Pelosi by the Arkansas man Richard Barnett; 60 as he posed with his feet on her desk only showed the highest degree of dishonour, and disrespect he had for law and order.

Yet, nothing really became of them except for a few arrests made. Again, and I will say that if these were Black people, the bloodshed would have been indescribable as they would have been shot like dogs on the streets.

Richard was jailed and yelled at Cooper that it was not fair that he was made to remain in jail while others were released. He should also scream that it was not fair that Donald Trump was acquitted, and he should also be shouting the question, where is Donald Trump when I need him?

How a Black man looking so casual got on the scene in Capitol Hill? It was a stark difference to the other Black man here, Emanuel Jackson was present at the January 6th insurrection. He forgot the rules of the game. Blacks will not have the same luck as his White Brothers. More than likely, he does not even know that he is from Jacob's tribe.

It was, therefore, of no surprise that this 20-year-old guy who was captured with the image of a metal bat was denied bail however, his white brothers, who some of them did the same damage, and much worse were granted release.

Yes, he had used that metal baseball to hit a row of police officers who were holding up Plexiglas shields, but his counterparts were the same or worse, but they were not faced with five federal charges, including assaulting an officer with a deadly weapon. I am not condoning his act because, in my mind, if you did the crime, then you must do the time. My argument here is that there was no fairness with the deliverance of punishment.

So many of Emanuel Jackson's race have said as well that it happened to him. What was he doing there in the first place? Some even justified their delight in his punishment because they deemed him as a sell-out, but I will never hasten to bring down my own brother like that. Donald Trump brainwashed many of those same White people who were present. Many have said that they regretted what they have done. He was 20, and many 20 years old will get into these situations because they cannot think before acting.

He has become a victim like many of his white brothers and sisters. They do not understand that the elites do not like any of them and do not care about them going to war whether this is at Capitol Hill or on any battle as long as they benefit from their slave mentality. As long as they profit from both sides of the war that they usually invest in. As long as their agendas are met and in this case; creating a reset that involves a cashless society, a new world order and most importantly for them, stopping that transitional power from Esau to Jacob's children. They are doing everything in their powers to stop it but pity them the fool.

It is fair to say then that Donald Trump did an excellent job for his foolish master, and one term was sufficient because they got what they wanted, and the game must go on. You see, time is of great essence. In the same manner that Pope Benedict had to swiftly go for the Jesuit Pope Francis to take over, although Donald Trump tried to slow it down, he still had to go making way for the next actor, and his name was Joseph Biden. Of course. Joe Biden, like the others, had to fit the criterion according to circumstances and the script. The stage is now being set since the biggest deception that the world has ever seen for that great deceiver whom I believe is amongst us today.

Joe Biden was 78 years old, many say that he has been showing signs of dementia, and let us be frank, he won't necessarily stand the test of time, which makes it easy for him to have a proxy government and so you just never know who is leading behind the scene. Very bitter to take in, but we must admit this possibility.

Joe Biden would make the perfect way for the appearance of the anti-Christ, whom I believe is amongst us at this very moment as the motions of the policies of the New World Order is underway. I met a young Black Hebrew Israelite by the name of Yawasap or Joseph along the High street of Seven Sisters. He called me out for eating a piece of chicken as I was walking and minding my own business. He was chastising me in love to forbid me from eating chicken. I knew that he was 100% right.

On my way back, I saw him still there on the corner spreading the good word. He drew me in, and on a different level, he was speaking to me regarding the end times. I was truly inspired by what he said to me, still nothing was more profound to me more than he shared with me an interpretation of the relationship between Donald Trump, Bill Gates, Barack Obama, and Joseph Biden.

He said that Bill Gates is the manufacturer, Donald Trump is the broker, and Obama is the salesman. He went on further to say that Obama was the boss of Joe Biden, and he still is, so you can only imagine what is going on behind the closed door. Yawasap was poignant with such a great analogy used. I was left fascinated by such great insight. He was spot on, except that I would say that Obama is more than a salesman, meaning he was able to take the souls of humans with his oratory skills. He was right, but Obama has a role that I believe is bigger than you and I, which leaves us to wait and see.

Yawasap was so modest not to claim what he knew, but he honoured the Most High for everything and credited his friends for the information he shared with me. In essence, he believed that the anti-Christ is here this minute and that we are somewhat aware but are not being able to handle this reality yet. Well, what do you think, because I know what I think?

Yes, I said it; I believe that the anti-Christ is here, and already we are feeling the pain as we are all sitting ducks, not knowing where to turn.

Let us face it as I reiterate here. Joe Biden is leading a proxy government.

Can you imagine the President calling Kamala Harris President in one of his presentations? He does not know who he is or even where he is. This type of problem spells real trouble because it is only a matter of time before the real player shows up. The crazy thing about it all is that there is nothing that we can do about it; except to take it as it comes, prepare for the worse to suffer and die. Some of you will say, what about your faith, and I will tell them that Yahuah warned us that many would die in my name. I always tell people that all except for one of Yahua's disciples were martyred. The one who was not martyred was John, who wrote Revelation, so what sayest though me? This is where we are at now and ten times worse is on its way, so just brace yourselves. Brace yourselves for the worse to come.

Chapter 9

Enemies Within

Let My People go.

There are many blacks who, when they see a Black brother or sister they feel comfortable and at home. For some, when they see a White brother or sister, they feel anger, hate, and in many cases, anxiety. However, some of those same Black brothers will serve and even push their brothers over to get the love of their White brother. On the other hand, these same Black brothers and sisters would rather support any other race but their own, and when they need help, the first one that these sorry excuses of Israelites run to is the same Israelites. Interestingly, they always get that help from the same Black brothers that they always scorn. It is a catch 22 because when you do support these Black brothers and sisters only to learn later that they would never touch you and only have an interest in other race; particularly the White race. This is why many Blacks refuse to get involved with their kind, even supporting them, and the vicious cycle continues. I totally get it because I have seen it over and over and over again.

For now, though, I speak on the case of those who feel comfortable when they see another Black brother. I have one word for you. Beware!

Always be on guard and never allow your race to define you. The second you allow your race to define you, then you will become the most vulnerable human being on this planet. Always see beyond the race of people and just remember that you can never truly see the hearts of a man. Their minds are their hearts, and this is what you can never see, but the Most High can.

Another Black man smiling with you does not necessarily mean that he loves you or cares for you, and the same can be said for all races. Some Black men and women supported Donald Trump and the Capitol Insurrection, however not all who supported him had the same reasons. Some supported him because they did not believe that the Democrats stood for them and that, in many cases, were true. Some are more in partnership with any side to destroy the

Hebrew Israelites, and they know exactly who they are. I must also make it clear that there has been talk that the Republicans have always been for the Black people and not the Democrats, there is some truth in that when you think of the fact that the Democrats fought the Republicans tooth and nail to continue enslaving us even after the abolition of slavery. Even the KKK, and it has gotten the Democrats written all over it. Nevertheless, I will say that none of them are good for any Black people. They are two of the same wings, left and right and they both want us all dead.

For many, especially those who unwittingly and naively think that all Blacks are the same if only walls could talk. I call those Black men who hate other Black men and women the enemies within the States.

There are some leading Black men behind the scenes who are destroying other Black people, and you would never have guessed that these were the enemies of the race. They are the ones who were the most friendly, helpful, and as a matter of fact, the most defensive of the Black race, but they are butchering us with the hands of other race and people, and you would never have guessed.

Fred Hampton is and will never be a Black Messiah in my eyes, in fact I find it blasphemous to use such a title when that title only belongs to Yahua Yahushua Messhiach, but Fred Hampton was gunned down only because of betrayal by his own Black brother; William O'neil, and there are many William O'neils amongst us. I will reiterate that anyone who tries to save Yah's people like this will pay a heavy price. Do not take my word for it; look at the record, and to add insult to injury, they have had the audacity to call Fred Hampton Messiah. I had to do a retake on that one. Outrageous!

Their reasons for killing and hating us vary, but I will share my views on the ones who are almost undetectable, well undetectable for some, not all. You see, you can fool some of the people some of the times, but you can never fool all of the people all of the times.

Do not get me wrong; some are destroying and killing other Black men in plain sight and do not care that you know them. I refer to Northern Nigeria as an example where the Christians are being slaughtered, and nothing has been done about it, but that is for later.

I believe that the spirits of the good and the bad live on for thousands and thousands of years, and as generations are passed on, the bad spirits pass on the hate or the need to settle that score. That spirit of hatred is shown through the humans' minds and actions, and this sometimes explains why some people will kill others and for, the passerby, they can never understand the reasoning behind the massacres ever so often in different places.

Take for instance the Hebrew Israelites who were made as slaves for 430 years in about the period leading up to 1304 BC under Pharaoh Seti before the exodus of our Black Hebrew Israelites about the time of 1304 – 1237 BC under the Pharaoh Rameses II.

In order to get a glimpse of what these rulers in Egypt might have looked like, I would like to share with you the most recent scientific findings of their appearances. The rulers that were years before Seti and Rameses II would have been the Egyptian King Akhenaten and Queen Nefertiti, who ruled about the time 1351 – 1334 BC.

Using Artificial intelligence, the Dutch photographer Bas Uterwijk released the modern images of the Egyptian King Akhenaten and Queen Nefertiti. If you look at the image, you will see that these were Black people.

The Black Hebrew Israelites were slaves at the time. These were the same Black people freed by the Most High who used Moses to let his people go. The same people who Yah said would return to Egypt, meaning bondage by ships. Are we not those same people? Yes, we are, and again if you read Deuteronomy 28, you would be further enlightened. Those same people were carried back into Egypt or by bondage in 1619 as slaves into the Americas and Europe.

I must point out that there is conflicting information amongst Historians and Archaeologists with one who has a totally different take on the period and even the names of the Pharaoh who were ruling during the enslavement of the Israelites. Archaeologists have said that Neferhotep I ruled during the 13th Dynasty when Moses was born and that Khaneferre Sibbekkotep IV was the step father of Moses when Moses had to flee to Sinai. They have further stated that Dudimose was the 24th King, and he was the Pharaoh of the exodus when the Israelites left Egypt for the Promised Land. The confusion is real, but the one thing that we can agree on is that the Pharaohs during Moses time and during the slavery of the Israelites were all Black people.

Some of these Pharaohs were Nubian Kushites, and some were Libyan Kushites and, for most, Hamites, but definitely were set apart from the Black Israelites.

So look at the images of the Egyptian King Akhenaten and Queen Nefertiti and take a very long good look at what our enslavers during Moses' time would have looked like. It does not matter if they were the actual rulers at the time, but they would have looked like any of the other Pharaohs. They were not Whites or Arabs but Black people. Today, with modern technology, we can easily separate them from the enslavers and the slaves.

They were destroyed and removed by Yah since the exodus for more than 120 years but do not for a minute think that they have never been active and amongst us today. They are the same today; the only difference is that they are not known by most today, but they are coming out of their hiding places. Their 400 years are up, and they are being smoked out. They cannot hide for too long now behind other races or people. I believe that the spirits of these Pharaohs lives on today and look the same way, but our Yah shall never forget and he is saying to them, 'Let My People Go.'

Whether they have taken a different form or hidden behind the children of Esau, Yah is still saying to them and is also showing it:

'Let My People Go.'

They are of the same hue today, and it is only a matter of time before the sheep will be separated from the goats. The Hamites and the Shemites will be known within this generation and will not be confused one for the other. Both Black people, but one is Israelite, and the other is not.

We will give a glimpse of these imitators hiding behind the black race, and we are going to smoke them out by their deeds and see if you can spot the ones I speak of here.

Let us look at slavery first because too often, the White men are given the total blame for Trans-Atlantic Slavery. However, if we are to be true to ourselves, we will accept that it was the chiefs in the villages of Africa who had assisted in the capture of the Africans who were the Shemites. They knew who the Shemites were because the Shemites were strangers in these African countries, mixed with the Hamites after they were forced into Africa.

The Israelites had to run from Jerusalem into Africa, India, and to the Mountains. So from 70AD, we the Israelites (Blacks who were for the most part slaves) had their tribes, and Titus Vespasianus Augustus would have known where they had gone because it was under his army that he invaded Jerusalem and massacred the Black Hebrews.

He would therefore know exactly where the diaspora would be located, and worse the Romans would have known all about their culture and history. They would know enough about them to return for them 1689 years later. Sure, for the most part, the whites played a vital role, as we can see here, but I reiterate; they were not alone.

The Hamites captured the Israelites in their villages for the Portuguese and many other Europeans, including the British.

It started with the Berbers informing the Portuguese about these strong Black men who were now in Africa because of Titus Vespasianus Augustus, who had chased them from Jerusalem. In many cases, the nobles of these chiefs were captured themselves and taken into slavery. Let us look at some examples here.

The enslavers themselves becoming enslaved themselves with the Congo Empire being a prime example.

Some might think that the Atlantic Slave Trade was chaotic, but it was not in the slightest. It was the most organized activity ever as for starter it was one of the prophecies of the Most High. Starting with the nomads from North Africa who informed the Portuguese about these strong black men who could be made slaves.

By the time it got to this stage, African regions such as the Congo Empire were well in the act.

King Mvemba Nzinga had dealings with the Portuguese. It was big business for the Congolese empire to trade us with the Portuguese.

The crazy thing was that they were trading us for simple thing things like mirrors, gun powder, and all those other outdated goods. Things got out of hand though because sooner than later and King Mvemba wanted to put an end to it all. He realized that they were not just us Shemites; their enemies but his own ethnic group and his own Royal family members.

Nzinga had this to say in a letter to a Portuguese King:

"Each day the traders are kidnapping our people, children of this country, sons of our nobles and vassals, even people of our own family. This corruption and depravity are so widespread that our land is entirely depopulated. We need in this kingdom only priests and school teachers, and no merchandise, unless it is wine and flour for mass. It is our wish that this kingdom not be a place for the trade or transport of slaves. Many of our subjects eagerly lust after Portuguese merchandise that your subjects have brought into our domains. To satisfy this inordinate appetite, they seize many of our Black free subjects...They sell them. After having taken these prisoners (to the coast) secretly or at night...As soon as the captives are in the hands of White men they are branded with a red-hot iron."

Now, Nzinga, isn't Karma a bitch! The evil and hypocrisy of this man. This part of his letter hit me like a ton of bricks.

'This corruption and depravity are so widespread that our land is entirely depopulated'.

Nzinga, you accused the Portuguese of being corrupt and depraved, but it was under your own regime that you were selling the Israelites for outdated goods.

Was that not corrupt and depraved, selling your own human race, never mind the colour of their skins or even their nationalities. You had forgotten what the bible had said in

Exodus 21:16

"Whoever steals a man and sells him, and anyone found in possession of him, shall be put to death".

Well let us see what history has shown us and you will see what happened to the Congo because most people never realised why the Congo has seen the worst atrocities mankind has ever seen on the face of this earth and never think to research and see that Yah's words never falter.

Let it never be said that the Hamite spirits of Egypt King Akhenaten (Amenhotep IV) or King Mvemba Nzinga and manyof the same have died. Their spirits; although since about or more than 3350 years ago, yet they live on to this very day with a hatred that is perhaps that it ever was.

King Leopold II was their worst nightmare. He was worse than Hitler or Stalin. In the late 1800s where King Leopold II killed more than 10 million Congolese.

I am in no way condoning what he did by committing genocide or cutting off numerous hands for those who did not yield enough rubber from the tree, but I am merely showing you that no one can or will escape their wrong deeds. They stole us for the Europeans and since then, they themselves were made into slaves and were killed more than any other nation. You should also realize that all is not as it appears. Many who have not a clue as to why they have had such consequences wail on how the White man is so wicked, but fail to realize the details in the devil. If we look close enough we will see that within the Black race, the enemies are most times black themselves and are hiding behind the least expected.

Let us not get it twisted thinking that although many of the enslavements happened with the Blacks in the Congo Empire that it was only in Congo Empire that was involved. Although I will show other examples of Congo, I shall show different examples of the other Hamites at work.

Their hatred is manifested today against the same Black Shemites that resulted in the Capitol insurrection and we will see that it is the Shemites to this day who are always targeted. Think about it, not all Blacks are of the same target or tribulations. The same tribe that has been singled out since they ran from Jerusalem are the same tribe that has been described in Deuteronomy 28:68 that Yah told Moses would return to Egypt, meaning bondage in ships.

Deuteronomy 28:68 (King James Bible)

"And the LORD shall bring thee into Egypt again with ships, by the way whereof I spake unto thee, Thou shalt see it no more again:

and there ye shall be sold unto your enemies for bondmen and bondwomen, and no man shall buy you."

All of this was prophesized and has happened, so the blame is not completely on the Whites or anyone else, but there is a consequence for everyone and since the 400 years of that curse is up, then it is payback time now although some of the enemies have partially had their consequences.

It was, therefore no coincidence that Congo experienced the atrocity worse than any other nation or country has ever endured.

The Hamites came from all over Western Central Africa, where most of our Black Israelite Brothers and Sisters ran to.

Think about it, Benin was an area of Hamites that was called the Kingdom of Judah. This alone proves to you that we escaped to different parts of Africa and we thought we were safe but we were right in the enemies' hands.

Look at part of this British map of 1747 showing the disputed location of the Kingdom of Judah as we currently know it to be Benin.

Disputed because there are conflicting views that this place was never a place where the Israelites fled to or named after them. They further debate that the name Juda was merely based on the language of the French and the Portuguese and that in any case the Portuguese named it Ajuda to reflect the word and its meaning; help because the Whydahs were slave catchers for the Portuguese and nothing else.

Well, if I am to examine this further, I doubt that not all Hamites will tell the truth as this is a stain on their history forever. They will forever be in denial that they were the enemies within, the traitors for life so I would never take for gospel what any of them has to say. Besides, they being known as the catchers speaks volumes about just who they were. In any case, I see it clear and plain Kingdom of Juda. Not Ajuda, but Juda and placing on the map, the Kingdom of helpers would just be simple stupidity. Which Colonizer is going to put their enemies on a pedestal to tell the world that they were helped by their enemies? Absolutely not. They will always want the entire praise for themselves.

It is very complicated, but to this day these traitors are working hand in hand with different nations and between themselves, Black Hamites, White Japhethites, and Arabs all fighting against that one common enemy of theirs; the Shemites.

With technology, they can work in greater unison and still be invisible to all of us but they still believe that they are invincible so they are working harder than before. So not because we did not see the Hamites at the Capitol insurrection means that they did not have a role to play.

Let us look on other examples now then, shall we?

Prince Abulrahman Ibrahim Ibn Sori was a Prince from the modern day Guinea; West Africa. His father was a ruler of the area in 1776 (same year USA gain its independence). Where his son lived and studied. Abdulrahman was very intelligent, a well learnt African who spoke four different languages and could read and write in Arabic.

During one of Abdulrahman military campaigns he was captured and sold into slavery. He was sold to the British who brought him to Mississippi where he laboured on the cotton plantation of Thomas Foster for about 40 years. He wrote a letter to his relatives in Africa and a Dutch man named Andrew Marshal sent the letter to the US senator and at the time Thomas Reid gave the letter to the US consulate in Morocco since the US government was assured that Abdulrahman was a Moor. After the Sultan of Morocco read the letter, he asked President Adams and Secretary of State Henry Clay to release Abdulrahman, and a few years later, Prince Abdulrahman was released.

There you go. They have always worked together and they; the Arabs, Whites, Hamites (Blacks who hate the Black Shemites) all have one thing in common; and that is hating on the Shemites. The enemies within protect each other. (A perfect example to the Capitol Hill Insurrection is where the far right group Proud Boys were heavily supported by the American Chinese. 80 % of the funds sent to the proud boys came from the American Chinese. Why am I not surprised that behind the scenes, they are completely united against us. And yet they are now calling foul, racism and even got a bill to protect them. If they think that Kamala Harris can save them now that the 400 years are up, they will soon learn that they are completely mistaken).

Never forget that the Arabs had the Blacks as slaves and even treated the Shemites worse than their European counterparts. Now here is a good one:

Princess Anta Madjiquene Ndiaye Also known as Anna Kingsley Anta was a Princess of the Wolof people of modern day Senegal. At the tender age of 13, she was captured and sent to Cuba where she was purchased by Zephaniah Kingsley, a slave trader and plantation owner of the Spanish colony of Florida. During this time, her region was in constant warfare, and slave raids were a great threat for everyone in the region. Her life was pretty much the point of this chapter because she went from being Princess to a slave owner herself. You got that right; there were a few Black slave owners in the USA; both males and females during the height of slavery.

At the age of 18, she was freed, but that did not stop her from having responsibilities on the plantation in East Florida. Overtime, she managed a large plantation and became the personal owner of 12 slaves herself. She died at the age of 77 years of age. She would have owned mainly Shemites and even if she did not, how much more treacherous could she be of being a slave and then becoming a slave owner herself.

Here is another one; William Ansah Sessarakoo. He was the son of John Corrente who was the leader of the Anomabo's government and chief caboceer. William's father was a chief official of supplying enslaved Africans to Europeans. Overtime, European power became interested in gaining access to the wealth of Anomabo. His father wanted his son to get educated in England and more importantly, build relationships with England. The man entrusted to send William to England, instead betrayed his father and sent William to Barbados as a slave. Years later, a Fante trader happened to see William in Barbados and quickly alerted the authorities of his son's fate. The British were petitioned to free William and the Royal African Company and the English Joint Stock Company operating the slave trade liberated William and transported him to England. In England William was received as a Prince and gained the respect of London's high society. I can only imagine how many of the children of Jacob were thinking that Yah was on this serpent's side when really he was a part of the devil's arms.

This is why we should always be weary of what someone has because we just never know where or how they got it. We shared the same race but they were our enemies from day one. On the surface it would appear as if they share our sorrows and grief yet they were actually the ones who created our sorrows and grief.

Now you know why some Africans hate Black Americans so much. The Europeans are not worried about those children of Jacob who are in the USA and think that Africa is a safe haven, just be careful where you are going because their spirits have not changed one bit.

Then we had King Takyi of Ghana, yes Ghana where everyone seems to be running to. King Takyi was a ruler or chief of the Fante people of Central Ghana. Fante people again! He was a warrior. He sold some of his rivals; the Ashanti and others into slavery as captives to the British. Like others as we have discussed, but by no means a coincidence since Yah is in full control, he himself became enslaved. King Takyi was taken to Jamaica where he conspired with Queen Nanny to take over the Island in a war with the British.

In 1760, Chief Takyi and his men started a revolt at their local plantation killing the owners. Many slaves joined in King Takyi's rebellion, however; King Takyi was later hunted and killed and the rebellion was eventually put down. I grew up in Jamaica and learnt about King Taki and Nanny, in fact Nanny is one of our heroes. If I had learnt about the other side of Takyi whilst in school, I would have made an informed decision not to have recognized Nanny as one of my heroes or Takyi because at the end of day it was all about saving their own skins as Takyi was originally a sell out from day one and many Jamaicans have the same belief of Nanny due to the peace treaty that she and the rest of her cronies signed in 1739.

All of this to me reiterate the fact that our own or so we thought because we now known that the only thing we shared was the colour of our skins but we were different people in terms of identity they were sell outs. They were not Hebrew Israelites but Hamites and if you think that their spirits are gone, then you are sadly mistaken. They will turn on us again with the teaming of their European counterparts so be very careful especially at this moment in time.

As I have said before; what has struck me most here is that many, particularly the American Blacks are running from the madness in the States to places like Ghana and some other parts of Africa, not realizing they are running straight in the arms of the number one enemies. The very ones who sold us in the first place and when the time is right will turn on us again. This time it will be even more deadly than our fore-parents who went through slavery. We will be trapped like never before, but I remember correctly, this is where Yahua Yahushua Messhiach will save us in the most miraculous way again as he has done before. If nothing else just remember this one thing, they are no different today as they were then.

There were many more who had supplied African slaves to the White Europeans. Our number one enemy which is Esau children and for many were captured themselves but released once they were proven not to be Jacob's children but Hamites. The enemies within are at this moment committing genocide of our people and we are not aware because they are of the same Black colour and so we are confused pondering just why do we hate our own so much, but they are not our own.

They are more in unison with the Europeans and that is why not all Blacks are killed by their police the same way. The enemies within have always had a happy ending; at least for now because the tide is swiftly turning, and they know it. It has been 400 years now, and so their time is up! One last example; I think that it is best ending with another Congolese Ganga Zumba.

Ganga Zumba was a first leader of a massive runaway slave settlement in Brazil. Zumba was an enslaved African who escaped bondage from a sugar cane plantation and eventually rose to the position of the highest authority literally creating his own kingdom in Brazil. He got the title Ganga Zuma, meaning great lord. He was of African Royalty, being the son of a Princess from the Congo Empire. Let us not forget that this same Congo Empire was instrumental in capturing other Black Africans for the Portuguese. Remember King Mvemba Nzinga, who wrote that letter when he realized that his own family was being captured amongst Jabob's children. Well, at some point, there was a war between the Portuguese and the Congo Empire. It was during the warfare with the Portuguese, the battle of Mbwila when Ganga Zumba was captured as a prisoner of war and sent off to Brazil.

Please take note that the Battle of Mbwila brewed from the Portuguese pressing claims over Southern Vassals of Kongo, particularly the country of Mbwila.

Mbwila was a nominal vassal of Kongo which had signed a treaty of vassalage with Portugal in 1619. Take note of the year 1619 because this was the official start of slavery of our people. Anyway, Ganga helped to form rural communities of former slaves from Africa in Brazil, which later formed intoa well organized kingdom in which he became King. By the 1670s, Ganga Zumba had a Palace, three Wives, Guards, Ministers, and loyal subjects at his Royal compound called Macaco. The compound consisted of 1500 houses which had houses family, guards and officials all of which were considered Royalty. It was so fitting that a Royal of the Congo Empire would continue his elevated lineage by literally creating an empire of his own under the worst conditions possible. It would not however, be fitting if he were a Shemite as he not live as he curse was described onto us in Deuteronomy 28. There is nothing about Ganga Zumba for us to feel proud of or honoured about. Until we start to recognize who we are as a people and that we are separate and apart, only then shall we be truly free.

They were never our Kings or Queens, and this is the time for us to recognize that fact instead of calling the true and genuine ones like myself sell-outs when we call out our enemies for who they are while they hide behind the one thing that we have in common and that is the colour of our skins. Never mind, because the Most High will do what must be done by himself. He will soon separate the wheat from the tare, and being that we are in the last days the truth shall come out, and everyone will know who is who. No one shall escape as the truth is already coming out in plain sight. You cannot forever hide behind being Black as your enemies who are also Black. It is only a matter of time before all is revealed.

Many will say that I am buying into the narrative of self-hate and complete division, but I will say to them he who feels it knows it. The division was there long before the White man came on the scene but was adapted and developed by the European and as I have shown they work in partnership with our main enemy who happens to be the children of Esau.

The time of playing stupid and sleeping with our enemies is over now. We do not have to because the

400 years is up, and now every man is for himself, so you can forget about the race cards now. Race should be playing a minor role because it is more of a spiritual war like it has always been, but we would be foolish to rule out the part that race plays in further destroying every one of us, but more so the Shemites.

The Capitol insurrection has everything to do with this because if the truth is told, those same Hamites had a strong role to play in the enslavement of the Black Shemites by unifying with the Europeans, some by greed and some by force. These Hamites are the puppeteers of today, pulling the puppets' strings, such as Donald Trump. The Capitol Insurrection was just a distraction or deflection towards the actual outcome that they desire, and that is to make us all slaves again, this time under complete control with the ultimate aim of bringing their master in place for worship. It is however written, they will all be crushed just as they were at Red Sea. This time though the leader, Yahua Yahusha Messhiach; of the Shemites, and all who have become part of the vine will protect all that is with him, and although they will suffer and die, their eternity will be one of tranquility like no one has ever experienced.

We are wising up, whether you want to believe it or not, so I will leave you with one message as the Most High instructed to tell that Pharaoh, Let My People Go.

The enemies within are very much our own as well. No one will be spared as I share with you the root of our problems.

Within our own, we have the greatest issue of our people; the children of Jacob who have internally destroyed us again, again and again.

Let us start with the Missing Fathers. In Jamaica, it all evolved from the dance hall songs, through the words, where young men were forced to have sex with dozens of women to prove that they were men and not gays. Ironically, some of these men were gays anyway, but they had to prove otherwise. The problem with this was that it became a vicious cycle with more significant issues for our people. These 'girly men' were manufacturers of gays or machines for producing many gays, and so a lot of closeted gays were the end product of the dance hall songs.

Not only that, they have created monsters whose hatred for women has now led to the continuous murders of our children and beautiful women in some of the most horrific manner. Added to that, gangs were increased with the advent of seeking father figures. The atrocity never ended there. In London, it is documented that these gangs have been raping the young boys as revenge for shortening their returns; in some cases, I have learned that this was done on purpose to ensure that these young Black and White boys remained in the gang and become submissive to the gang. It is my sincere belief that if the positive father figure were there in the first place, then these vulnerable young Black youths and White youths would not be in this state of mind.

Some men have looked at these scenarios and have said that they would never be caught in that situation. I say, for some, maybe so, but when a mother is left alone to house, clothes, and feed her children with no father figure then, anything is possible. It is these same young men who are caught in the net and end up in prison. This is where the vicious cycle continues because those same men leave prison and ends up

175

doing the same to their children, and so the generational curse continues upon the fourth and fifth generation.

We then become targets for everyone to piss on. The prison system feeds off us, the educational system feeds off us, and the political and economic system feeds off of us. It is no wonder that Trump and his envoys are always using us for their propaganda tool. That is because we have been weak, and they have so much to gain from us, and we have nothing to gain from them but sorrows. If I were Trump and saw that my wealth would continue to grow from the continuous exploitation of Black people, then perhaps I too would be accused of Capitol Insurrection. Let us face it, without the Black man, they would have nothing, so they will fight to the last drop of their blood to remain in that power.

Even the Asians set up their shops in the hood or ghettoes where we are. If we were that poor, why would they? They know that we will spend the money on them only and not ourselves so they set their businesses where we are. Their time is up too, and I think that they are realizing this very fast.

The fear of the Black man being the one to rule is like turning one on its head. It is like the impossible, but they know that it is imminent, and so it is most important to keep the negative social and economic narratives in place for the Black man. However, for a few shillings, some of our own have been sell-outs. Not living to their responsibilities makes you a sell-out. Singing songs that destroys your own kind, minds make you a sell-out, and selling narcotic drugs to your own or to anyone for that matter certainly makes you a sell-out.

When we turn away from the Most High's laws then we make our own weaker; making the enemies walk all over us. I believe that we are the most hated group of people ever to walk this earth, which is a fact. Just look at the racism that we have to endure irrespective of the country that we might visit. The hatred that we have shown for our kind is just unbelievable, never mind strangers hating on us. It leaves me to conclude that if ever we had a great enemy, we were the greatest enemies to ourselves; if ever there was an enemy within, we were our greatest enemy.

I shall reiterate that the singers have been instrumental in destroying the minds of our Black children, and they too shall pay dearly. I always wondered how it is that so many minds have been captured to do so many wrongs through singers. Then I remembered that satan was the lead singer. You can appreciate why singers are paid everything while Teachers and Nurses are never paid well. I also remembered that he is the current ruler of this earth for now and remember how he deceived Eve. He has been doing the same to this day. However, these traitors were very much aware of what they were doing when they destroyed this unique nation of Jacob. In most cases, their action was from pre-meditated acts anyway.

I will illustrate my point even further. I have personally known one of these same men who ran from his responsibilities and all because of selfishness, greed, and hate for the woman he claimed to have loved. He was the most arrogant, narcissistic liar that you will ever meet, surely a devil's whore.

This coward or forever a boy had another son in Jamaica in about 1969, and by 1970 he had another son with a different woman from which he ran, leaving the Mother and the son to suffer immensely. This has been the case for millions over hundreds of years, and in the event destroying the foundation of the people.

There are many traitors like him, no different from Judas, and they all deserve the same fate as Yahua laid out for telling him that it would have been better if he had never been born. I say this without an apology because these traitors contributed significantly to the failures of many innocent Shemite Black brothers and sons, which have partially led to massive incarcerations, deaths, and worse of all, a continued subjection to the main enemy; the children of Esau. These traitors will pay dearly one way or the other in this world or the next.

I do not have to witness these coward's fate because Yahua is a living God, and he never fails. For some of the cowards, it was about their self-gratification and for most of them, nothing but being plain evil and thinking that they can get away with it. Well, your 400 years are up, and everything you owned will soon be of no value. Even the money in your bank account will quickly be of no value. You thought that ignoring your seed would save you money or make you rich so that you could boast and have that puffed-up chest to show the world. It is now 2021, and you are cornered! Where your pride now as there is no escape for you. The best part of it all is that you are oblivious to your condemnation.

If only they had followed the laws of Yah, then there would never have been such a mess amongst our people.

Chapter 10

No One Will Escape Punishment For The Black Man's (Shemite's) Pain NONE!

There is a saying; we are all Spiritual beings having a human experience. If only we humans realized this and, in the process, recognize that whatever affects one affects all. However, as Black Shemites, we have suffered through the revealed prophecy of Deuteronomy 28. We have been subjected to the hate and ridicule of all nations. Whether they were Chinese, Indians, Whites and even our own race Blacks along with the Shemites. Not once was any other nation concerned in one accord. Neither had any of them condemned slavery, oppression and murder of the Black nation, which was opened for all to see, instead, they became part of that problem. Yes, there have been some countries in recent times which have become more vocal against racism, but for many, it has been because their back is now against the wall, and they realize that the shift is totally going against them of which they can do nothing about. Also, they realize that they are next, so suddenly, they are joining in unison. However; not once did a nation condemned racism when it was rife in earlier times. During slavery times, you might try to argue with me on this matter. Do not come to me with the argument that the likes of William Wilberforce, Thomas Clarkson, or any other of the other so-called abolitionists were integral to abolishing slavery. Absolute nonsense.

They played a very insignificant part, especially at the most convenient time of industrialization when the machinery was more viable than the slaves themselves. Slavery was just not economically viable anymore, so the slave owners were experiencing more loss than gain.

It was not the British alone that have stood and gained massive wealth and power from the presence of the Black man and is about to reap what they have sown. Every other nation has a lot to answer because too many of them were silent killers and certainly, beneficiaries of Jacob's children. They became filthy rich from the Black man's suffering. No matter where we went, and they would poke fun at us. They called us names; they abused us and, they murdered our Children, our Mothers, and our Fathers. They never bought from us or traded with us, and they owned us; another human being. The tide is about to turn. It has been 400 years now! Yes, we will suffer a lot during the transition, but you shall see that the end result is real.

Yes! Have you not already noticed that because of Covid 19, with the apparent source being Wuhan, China, everything and everyone has been turned upside down?

How interestingly 2019, the end of the 400 years; that International trade was hit hard, and in more than 200 years, the GDP had an all-time low worldwide. International airports have been closed, jobs are gone forever, homes are gone, and everyone's freedom has slipped away. They are attacking everyone to secure their power because they just do not want to let go and transfer the power to their Black brothers. Do not get it wrong because I am in the mix, and I am feeling it too and will most likely feel it even harder than many, but I rejoice knowing what is to come at the end; if not for myself, my future generation.

Never mind all of that, let us justify why other races other than the White and Black men who have resulted in the Shemites suffering must pay as their consequences have already started.

Just to show how blatant and bold these people are, there is a store called the Nigger king clothing store in Taiwan. Can they get any worse than that? Let us not forget that during the Covid 19 hysteria when all eyes were on China, China tried that propaganda twist to turn all on Africa as if Africa started the Covid 19 and, subsequently, they evicted many Africans from their apartments. The Chinese had the Africans' passports taken from them and kicked them out into the streets of China.

China's racist and hatred for Blacks have always been known by just about everyone Chinese, Japanese, and Vietnamese all travel to Africa, and then they created billion-dollar empires. And in those empires, they have exploited the Africans, and at the same time, they never hired the Blacks. Even here in the UK, I have never seen any other race except their own working in any of their facilities. Who could ever forget the Art museums in China filled with pictures of monkeys, chimpanzees, and Apes all positioned beside Black people, all in the most distasteful manner to say that Blacks are Monkeys, Chimpanzees, and Apes? There is also the normality of Vietnamese and Koreans regularly colouring themselves in black faces on the televisions. This has always been embedded into the psyche of these people but their time is up, and the table is turning out of their favour. We must call a spade a spade, and you will see that even though it is always the White man that is shouted at for racism, the Asians are very much at the forefront, and most of them have always hated us, although they too can never do without us.

They like the White men, have always portrayed us Blacks as the stupid, lazy, and inferior ones; they never invented the stoplights, Railway signal, touch-tone telephone, Draftsman, Closed Circuit television security (the early form of CCTV).

IBM computer, pacemaker, the blood bank, animation on the web, online video, World's fastest computer, gas mask, traffic signals, tissue holder, sanitary belt, X-Ray spectrometer, Rotary engine, Letterbox, Ironing board, First steam engine for a ship, lawn mower, train alarm, peanut butter, shutter, elevator, ventilation aid, riding saddles, shoe, door knob, guitar, golf tee, cabinet bed, motor, lamp, Bicycle frame, swinging chairs, air conditioning unit, printing press, fire extinguisher, lock, cooker, horseshoes, attachment for lawn mowers, airship, scaffold, folding chairs, baby buggy, hoister, comb, refrigerator, mop. I am tired, so I will stop there. So the next time any of you think that you invented anything, just remember what you sit on or use because a Black man invented all of that. As for the rest of you, the only thing that you have invented, and that has been lies and deception. You got that right; you are the masters of deceptions, but all those lies are being unveiled, and soon you will be naked for all to see as it has already begun.

Now let us get back to the matter at hand. Again I shall continue with China because they are the wannabe that will go down very quickly.

For all those who believe the fallacy that China will be the next world power, think again. Even now, with the pretence that China is the next super power with a threat to take over from the USA is nothing but a joke. Yes, it is true that China is the world's largest producer of steel, world's largest textile and clothing industry, one of the world's largest trader with trillions of dollars in foreign trade as a major overseas investor as they take Africa by a storm and one of the main arms dealers in the world. With all of that, I still maintain that this does not make them the next superpower to take over from the USA. They are the most suitable to be used to manipulate and put in place the infrastructure for the most sinister agenda that the world currently faces. However, once China has done what the system requires, they will be disposed of as if they had never existed. In fact, no country is indispensable. Not even the USA because they all have a role for the bigger picture, and once they have been used then the shout will be 'next'.

You see, one of the importance of China is that it is used as a model, or for a better word, the guinea pig for the wider world. In that world, it is complete totalitarian, and they standardize the assessment of their citizens and businesses credit, be it their economic or social reputation.

That model of totalitarian is being rolled out to the wider world. Besides, stealing the resources of Africa and making Africans' lives hell will soon be a thing of the past as Africa is uniting and wising up. African leaders are bonding together against China, and many have alleged that the latest Tanzanian President was poisoned due to his stance against allowing his country to be exploited of its resources. The speculation of his death will only strengthen the resolves of all African leaders, with the Ghanian President taking the lead. China will soon have no foot to stand on. I would not be surprised if the might of the USA and the UK steps in to support Africa. These two power countries see China as a threat more now than ever before and have already flexed their muscles to pull

China down even to ensure that the end game for the reset, agenda 21 and, New World Order is achieved. We are already seeing the start of China being disposed of since the virus was set up to start in Wuhan. That was not just a social, and economic disruption for China but also a political disruption to the max. Besides, Donald Trump had already started that economic disruption with the trade war against China with the tariff war that has displaced many business, especially small businesses in China and now with an impending attack on China with Boris Johnson and Joe Biden, I am certain that China will go further into the abyss.

The same system is then rolled out to the wider world as you can see that the world has become a totalitarian system now through the use and excuse of Covid 19 and its lockdowns. China is the perfect guinea pig for this since it is also a country with the broadest social inequality in the world.

They spread their wings with the same ideology and principle on the continents of Africa and the Caribbean, amongst other places. It is however, not far-fetched to see that China is a pawn in the game of the wider system called the new world order. Esau's children are in control of them, and they have no choice on the matter. China appears to be the new colonizers, but if you follow the trend closely, you will realize that they are only being used to develop the infrastructures of the poorer countries. Sure there are other major interests of China, but one of their main activities has been to develop the infrastructure. All being done to ensure easy accessibility and consequently paving the way to reach the people who, in the past, would have been difficult to reach. Once they have done their part and the control and manipulation of the people are done, it will be goodbye to China. Once Esau can ensure complete globalization to suit his agenda, then it is a goodbye to China. In fact, they have already started.

Lately and the West has been saying that China is their greatest threat. Talk like this will mean that an imminent attack on China is only a matter of time. The same way they have brought down Iraq, Libya, and Syria and soon, in the same way, they will bring China down. The tariff war between China and the USA was not enough to bring China down, but I am almost sure that China will soon be down. China has to be brought down before they can successfully bring their sinister agenda 21 in full mode, and for the sake of the reset, China will be put down like an injured animal. If you follow the current news, then you will see that the USA and the UK has already started the process of taking China down, and down they shall go.

Never before has China's reputation been such an open sore, they are now blatantly attacked on the streets of the USA. They have been physically and verbally abused on the streets. The Asian Americans are now unsafe in the streets, with women sadly being gunned down in places such as Compton, Los Angeles. Then there were six women gunned down in Atlanta, blatantly due to their race. It was reported that the perpetrator had blamed Asians for Covid 19. The attacks on both male and female Asians have been far greater than reported, and now many have come out to speak against Asian racism.

As much as I am against any form of racism, how different it would have been if Asians had employed Blacks in their restaurants, but although they might have done so, I have never seen this. How good it would have been if they had employed Blacks in the African communities instead of only including themselves in the resources they have taken over from another man's country.

How good it would have been if they were a voice to defend the Black community that they share in the USA. The Whites have marched and have spoken out against the injustice that have been meted out against the Black communities, but never have I seen any Chinese supporting our cause.

We now have racism in reverse and these same people who have looked down on Black people are now being told to go back to China, are being spat in the face, and all sorts. An old Chinese woman was attacked by a Caucasian man in San Francisco only for her to retaliate and interestingly leaving him on a stretcher and in Hospital. Her Grandson raised more than 800,000 dollars, and she refused the money and instead donated it to charity to fight against racism within the Asian community. Very noble of her, but I doubt that even a fraction of that amount would have been raised by any community for the Black Shemite being attacked due to racism. An African maybe, but not a Shemite.

I will reiterate that any form of racism is wrong, and as one human race, if we all equally attacked the demon of racism, then I would have respected all for their efforts. However, the Black people have always been treated by the wider society as if they deserved it and have never been defended in the way that it should. For that reason, I can see why every race, including the Black race, must give an account for the hate and murders that they have allowed to occur against the Black Shemites. So many innocent Black lives have gone blatantly in front of our eyes, and the sad part of it has been where many children and very young adult lives have been stuffed out all because they have been Black and then suddenly I must feel remorse for one or two victims of your race. Well, the 400 years are up, and no race will escape the consequences that they deserve.

All these countries and people who have contributed and looked away while we, the children of Jacob, were made slaves, persecuted, and murdered will get and have begun to get their just rewards. The time will come when you shall drink their blood and sweat that you took from us. Most of them exploited us, taking our energy and time and through the businesses of their false hair or wigs generating trillions for themselves.

Not to mention their bleaching products. This is where the Indians come in big-time now. Bleaching products for Black people also generates trillions for these so-called people who then have the audacity to look down on us! They have exploited us by using the emotional degradation and destruction of our self-esteem and self-worth caused from slavery and the curse that we have caused on ourselves by not following the laws of our God, The Most High Yah. Stupidly and they thought that they would get away with all of that, but alas! All of that wealth they have stolen from us will soon mean absolutely nothing to them as the settings are all in place for the transition of power to the Black Shemites. The cashless society will be their fate as they shall be doomed if they take that chip in their body, and most will take that chip or the mark of the beast, which will ultimately lead to their forever doom. You better enjoy it now while it last because it shall not last for much longer.

The very reason for the Capitol insurrection. A plot to distract and prevent the process of this transition. They cannot stop it, though, no matter what they do because as it is written, the first (Esau) shall be the last, and the last (Jacob) shall be the first. We are now the first in coming to roost, and no one on this planet can do jack about it. And for those who still cannot see how the Asians fit in here, let me remind you of the thousands in Tokyo who showed their support with many marches and rallies of Trump supporters against Biden's inauguration.

They were clearly in support of the Capitol Insurrection. Needless to remind you that these same Japanese were staunch allies of Adolf Hitler.

Chapter 11

Babylon is Falling!

Y ahua Yahushua Messhiach once said in Matthew 12:25 from the King James Version;

"And Jesus knew their thoughts, and said unto them, every kingdom divided against itself is brought to desolation; and; every city or house divided against itself shall not stand."

Well, we have been witnessing just that within the last kingdom of this earth; the British Royal family, as it appears to implode with Meghan Markle and Prince Harry being blamed as they have caused quite a stir.

The interview with Oprah Winfrey highlighted the cracks within that Royal family, with racism being the centre of its accusation. The power of Esau, the White man, has been in place above Jacob, the Black man for thousands of years even before the Greeks with

Alexander the Great, Romans, Ottoman, and now the British, the last one standing and yet falling.

Only a matter of time now, and I would not be surprised if the complete fall of Babylon comes within our sight in less than ten years. We will be bound to see the complete and possibly sudden departure of the British power and again to be kind ten years. They are already being destroyed from within.

It started before Meghan Markle, but with Lady Diana. You see, many believed that Prince Harry is really the father of James Hewitt, A British former Calvary Officer. The resemblance of Harry to James Hewitt as opposed to Prince Charles has made this rumour even more significant, but it has been a taboo that very few speak about. The truth is that, if this were to be the truth and were to be publicly known, then this would have been the last nail in the coffin for the Royals so as usual, it would have been better if it were lies hidden hence to continue as their recipe of survival. Well, everything about Esau has been based on lies, just like their master. Ironically, whatever the truth, it will be lies that they have survived that will pull them down.

From the interview, Markle never appeared to have received the memo that whether you are fully Black or even with just a drop of Black blood that the hate would still be real.

This is why I am so happy with the wisdom of the Most High. The Mark Of The Beast is perfect indeed for identifying the true feelings of those who love him or not. With the mark of the beast that has already begun, you must decide as to which side of the fence you belong to, and no one can sit on the fence. It will no longer be a case of Islam, Hinduism, Sikhism, Christianity, Judaism or any other religion. You are either on Yah's side or satan's side. End of discussion. So someone like Meghan might very well sit on the fence, or sit on Yah's side or even satan's side, and no one but herself knows whether or not she feels any love for the Black community. Not that it matters to me as I have already had my thoughts of her, and besides, we are at the point where irrespective as to where she sits, the Most High is using her for the ultimate cause, and that is all that matters. His wisdom never fails, and no one can ever override that truth.

The truth is that Yah decided over 4000 years ago how it all would have ended, and he also decided who would have been used to make this transition happen. However, let us look at the matter of race because it seems as if race is playing a key role in helping Babylon to fall. Well, it makes sense since Jacob was Black and Esau was White, or as the bible described him red and ruddy and they were fighting since they were in the womb of Rebecca.

Genesis 25:25 (King James Version)
25 And the first came out red, all over like a hairy garment; and they called his name Esau.

What would make Markle a controversial figure amongst some Black communities is that many have accepted and many have rejected her as being representative of them, and most certainly, most Whites would never claim her.

Whatever happens to her, in the end is none of my business as it will be between she and her creator, who is my Yah.

Remember, Yah can use anyone to fulfil his will, and he has done this with our people before. He most certainly did this with King Cyrus the Great, who was a Persian King. Cyrus the Great was even an anointed of God. Whether one wishes to accept Meghan or reject her is up to them, but one thing is for sure, and that is, she has been the best thing that has ever happened to us as a Black race in a very, very long time.

She has already proven her strength and power for the cause of the Black community by being a part of the Black Lives Matter, causing many of our enemies to be running, and it is my belief that the Holy Spirit is working with her in many ways. God certainly has a hand in her success for our cause so far.

One must concede when she could indirectly have the Society of editor Chief resign over a row over an unacceptable statement. Just a call and Piers Morgan had to go, and this will leave a stain on his record for good, but it will not destroy him, probably make him more money. She had so many going upside-down, and I do not think that she is done yet. You must give credit where it is due, and so far, the Most High is using her effectively, and yet a lot more is to come and not necessarily from her.

Again, no surprise because 400 years are up, and Babylon must fall. This is only the start, as the enemy will have push-backs at every corner they turn, and they will not win no matter what they do. Their time is up, and Jacob's children are ready and will rule with their leader Yahua Yahusha Messhiach whether they like it or not.

Just think about it all. So much has been happening all at once since 2019, like Covid 19. These things can't be all by coincidence. Just like that occurred during the advent of the exodus during Moses' time. We have had the Covid 19, which by the way stands for certification of vaccination identification, we have an impending Covid passport. Then there was Brexit which was clearly manipulated and came in existence because they needed to have their way without any hindrance from the EU, and as we can see, the EU has been their hindrance with the movement of the vaccination even with the Brexit in place.

However, more is at stake against the British people since Brexit with their freedom and democracy threatened now more than ever before. The AntiTrespass bill that will prevent the freedom to protest amongst other freedoms that we take for granted, leading to hefty fines and prosecution, shows you how desperate they are to keep their power, and with Brexit, they have the ability now as they have never had before. Remember how they used race, immigration and anti-Europe narratives to get Brexit. You can now see why they did all of that, even advertising propaganda on moving vans across the country that were downright racist. We are now in a totalitarian system. Meghan's interview disrupted the British Royals, Prince Andrew's accused of mingling with a paedophile, then there was Donald Trump, and another setback being the Capitol Insurrection. There were more such as natural disasters like we have never seen before, and there will be a lot more to come. These were all insight at their worse since 2019, so it cannot be by coincidence with supernatural implications. There is a force beyond us, and it is shouting loud and clear; "Let My People Go." If anyone cannot see the meaning of this phenomena, then you are not only blind, but also dead!

Let us Shemites, the true Israelites, never forget that the rulers of this earth, be it the Government or Royalties, are nothing but extension of satan, and that their power is foolishness, nothing compared to us or our leader Yahua Yahushua Messhiach. Their fear has made them so desperate because not only are they aware of what they have to lose, but also the everlasting punishment that awaits them for what they have done to us. We are coming from the line of King David and more than ever the King of Judah; Yahua Yahusha Meshiach.

They call themselves blue blood, but their blood has incest with all sorts of evil mixed. I would never want to be a part of their bloodline, even if they offered the entire Universe.

Babylon is falling, and you know it when you see that they synchrone their efforts across the world with the vaccinations, laws, and force. We expect far worse from them as they could be easily compared to a drowning man clutching at straws.

Chapter 12

Jerusalema

The time is ripe for all to come together as one spirit to worship and serve the Most High. It is what we were made for, and no one can stop that. It does not matter if you are Black, White, or Asian, we all belong to Yah. I know that in previous chapters, the Whiteman, Blackman, and Asians have been identified and criticized for slavery, racism, exploitation, and even killings of the Blacks; particularly the Shemites. I also made it clear that the Shemites has no one else but ourselves because if we had followed the laws of our leader then we would not have experienced all of these punishments. While it was deserving, those who afflicted us shall not get away at all. The other truth though, is that because Yahua came to this earth, the true Israelites have not been guiltless, and so all are opened to his Kingdom.

The previous chapters might have caused some distress and depression, but that was not the sole intention. I am not the one who created those darkest scenarios but you yourselves. We all did this to ourselves, but the ones that we refer to the most are those who have been hurting mankind just to save their own. In most cases, through complete greed and blatant selfishness. They never see themselves as souls but as the special ones, better than another, even wanting to be worshipped as gods. I have shown that everyone has contributed to the demise of the Shemite, including himself. We have all transgressed and have departed from our leader.

Now this is where Jerusalema comes in. After all, it is not all doom and gloom though, because most of us will be saved by the mercies and grace of the Creator, the Almighty and the Most High; Yahua Yahusha Messhiach.

With all these calamities around us, remember that the Most High said that when you see these things happening look up because redemption draweth nigh.

One of the most positive parts of this last generation is that the Most High will return within their time, and although many will not survive, those who survive will be enjoying what was intended from the beginning. Peace, love, happiness, and all that anyone could desire, and that is complete utopia.

Yes, Yahua will return to rule with an iron fist, but that is not to discount the Peace, love, happiness, and all that anyone could desire, and that is complete utopia as he reigns from Jerusalem. It is also prophesied that on his return all nation must visit Jerusalem and partake in the feasts; such as the feast of passover, sukkat and the feast of tabernacle. Sure there shall be more, however any nation that refuse to visit and there shall be no rain in their country or land.

Zechariah 14:17

And it shall be, that whosoever will not come up of all the families of the earth unto Jerusalem to worship the King, the LORD of hosts, even upon them shall be no rain.

Whether you want to believe this or not is up to you. However, all is in plain sight and even now, all the infrastructure, both physical and spiritual are being prepared for this reality to come. The mass exodus in the Middle East has not been happening for no reason, and soon the attack on Jerusalem will be imminent, removing anyone who never belonged there in the first place! Atheist, agnostics, and theist eat your hearts out as I show you at least one example of how it is already in plain sight with the song Jerusalema!

Is it any wonder then that the song Jerusalema in good time came to us on the 29th November 2019. You got that right, 2019, the year that marked the beginning of the Israelites freedom after 400 years.

How much more remarkable that this song that took the world by storm came at that time. The song came out of South Africa of isiZulu lyrics; a Bantu language of the Zulu. What makes this most remarkable was that the song came from a surprising group, the Zulus, where their traditional religion is of many deities, mainly associated with animals, but they led the song of harmony; Jerusalema. The song from DJ Kgaogelo Moagi, or Master KG sang by Nomcebo went viral during the isolation due to the lockdown by Covid-19.

The dance became so trendy that if you should go to Youtube and tap in Jerusalema with the name of any country and you will see just about any of the 195 countries of the world dancing to this song as if they were dancing for their lives. Well, I would suggest that they never stop dancing because Jerusalem is significant to everyone on this earth because, after the tribulation which has already begun, we all must visit Jerusalem where the Most High will rule from for the next one thousand years, and there he will teach us all from the beginning again.

I shall repeat, 2019 was the end of the 400 years since slavery in 1619 and for this song to culminate with 2019 is most significant for everyone.

The dance is so captivating with Austria, USA, Jamaica, Peru, Argentina, Australia, and all others, it shows just how much we all have in common as more spiritual beings than human beings as we dance with not a care in the world. You would never have thought that there was a pandemic that was killing people as was reported across the print, broadcast and internet media. The unity of so many different cultures dancing to one culture different from their own but with one message was just mesmerizing, to say the least. Children from different countries, different schools; the young and the old dancing as if it were a Jubilee. All dancing as one spirit is just beyond supernatural, and it was supernatural. Supernatural because it has given us a glimpse of everyone's future immediately after we have passed through this present-day tribulation. A tribulation that shall last for several years, if not more. It has been written that this will be the worse time ever since the creation of this earth and never again after. Not my words, but the Most High.

It is no surprise to me that the pain, suffering, fear, unwanted surprises, circumstances, cause, and success for us have come at this time.

Let us celebrate what is to come. Out with the old and in with the new that most of us who have trodden on so desire. All those houses that the so-called religious leaders could have built for their followers and instead put every penny in their pockets will no longer be a cry from the victims who shell the offering out to these evildoers who hide behind the name of the Most High. Homelessness will no longer be an issue, neither will there be hunger, crime, war, disease, unemployment, anxiety, fear, natural disasters, drug abuse, racism, and so many more that have been associated with evil. They will be all gone, well, at least for another one thousand years before the enemy returns, but only for a very short time, and then it will be eternal peace and Utopia that cannot be described. Ladies and gentlemen, this is not a fable or a made-up story. It is not long now before, and although the process has already begun and has been compared to birth pain because as redemption draweth nigh, so will our sorrows meaning many will die to the point where there will almost be no flesh left on this earth.

However, we know that a joyous moment is on its way, and that is why Jerusalema has been so viral, with the souls of all men rejoicing exceedingly.

The change will be most welcome, not by all but for those who desire freedom from oppression which is all that we have been experiencing in all governments of the world. Soon and there will be no need for a human King, Queen, Prime Minister, Presidents, or any other that described themselves as rulers. We will not need them anymore because Yahua

Yahushua Messhiach will be reigning from Jerusalem, and what a glorious day that shall be.

The gravy train for those undesirable humans who called themselves leaders will be gone, and good riddance, I shall say. Their power and enslavement over us, the normal humans, will not exist anymore and, will never return.

This is why we must all join in and sing Jerusalema

Here are the words in English:

Jerusalema

You are my home

I wanna be there

Back home to you

Don't leave me this way

Jerusalema

You are my life

I wanna be there

Back home to you

Don't leave me this way

This is not my place

This is not my realm

You will watch my steps

You will guide me here

You'll save my soul

Take me away with you

I'll find my way

I'll find my way

I'll find my way

Take me away with you

I'll be there for you

I'll find my way

The truth will win the day

I will be back to you

As The Most High strips every one of what they have got, whether it be your company, business, money, land, and even of yourself. there will be a breaking point, and you shall not be blaming Black Lives Matter, White Lives Matter, or anything else for that matter. Instead, every one of you, even the die-hearted atheist, agnostic, or theist, must do one thing! You will bow to Yahua, Yahusha Meshiach (Jesus Christ), and every one of your knees must bow and confess that he is the Lord, the beginning and the end, and to him alone all Glory belongs. Do not believe, just watch and see because that process has already begun! To all the leaders of the West, and the East I would suggest that you start running, but we know that you are the stupidest creatures to exist, so you will try to defend what does not belong to you with all you got from the return of the Most High but only to your death sentences. To show a simple parallel, it will be like President Donald Trump trying to stop the lawmakers from confirming President-elect Joe Biden's poll win.

Making that last speech and telling the people to march to Capitol Hill, only to lead to total disaster. The only difference here is that the result will be 10,000 worse for those deluded earthly leaders. It is already becoming a fatal one because for those who have not realized that the war is right in front of you with you being actively part of the war, then you better wake up. Yes, you are fighting a war and do not even realize it. Thousands have already died, some might say that it was the covid that killed them, but it is all part and parcel of the war my friends. Even before and increasingly since the increase in technology with the internet, they have zeroed in on you and enlisted you on a side. Yahua's side or satan's side. You are on one of the sides, but it will soon be as plain as A, B, C for all to see and know.

Monitoring our every move with the mobile phones, computers and all sorts such as CCTV amongst other big brother gadgets. They have ensured that our independence has been taken away from us by destroying the middle class. Teachers, nurses, and even the police have suddenly become the new lower class, many struggling to even pay the mortgage. The plan was to destabilize all our finances and making us entirely dependent on them or their system. Once they got us in their trap, those who they struggle to get will still break under their draconian laws that have rolled out from China's police state system and now an International system. The Geneva Convention will soon be gone, and effectively our human rights throughout the world will be gone, a thing of the past.

Not to worry, all this will soon be a thing of the past, this is why I will say. Watch the inspiring song Jerusalema.

The next seven years or more will be about total control as they will get into our minds by any means necessary. All this to ensure that they will keep the power that is slipping from their grip. They will take all wealth or belongings, and they must as even a child can now be wealthy from social media such as Instagram, WhatsApp, Tic Toc, Facebook, and it is changing every day.

Ironically, it is that same media that they have been using against us in order to trap us, making us in the place where we currently are. With their algorithms and artificial intelligence, they got us all in a cage or, for a better word. They got us all in a prison. They know everything about us. So now with complete confidence, they blatantly tell us that without the Covid passport you will not be able go to the Public House now, but soon and it shall be Cinemas, theatre, stadium, any sports events, and I will not be surprised in the least when this is further rolled out to supermarkets and schools or even work places. The scary part of this is that you will not be able to do squat about it. Thinking about traveling on the plane to Spain or anywhere else in the world without the Covid passport? Forget it. You will not be able to go anywhere or do anything. Our freedom has already been restricted for ages in the UK by way of expensive cost, but soon and it will not matter whether or not you can afford it. All of these actions and new laws all because they are desperate to keep their power and control and they are intent on ensuring that the power of transition does not go to the Black man, but how wrong they are.

What next after all of this then? Their desperation will lead to micro chipping all humans. Have you not noticed where their change is leading to? The virus is the current excuse. We do not want to spread the virus, so please do not hand us any money, better to use the card. They had this cashless society underway a long time now, but in recent times they have been talking about card less society. The only sound warning I can give here is that no one should allow themselves to be chipped, no matter the narrative that they might spin on you. It will be a very difficult one, especially when they will make it clear that without the chip, no buying or selling and in this world, even if you have your own, it will be almost impossible to ignore no buying or selling. Besides, if you should take the chip or the mark, it is clear that the Most High will want nothing to do with you in this world or the next. It would be over, finished, done!

It is a catch 22 as well because without it you won't even be able to eat. Well, those who have land to grow their crops and live like a subsistence family, then good for you, but even with that, you will at some point need the resources that the enemy has made us so reliant on. I therefore reiterate, do not take it!

I do not care what others think, but I am determined not to take it, and I pray that the Holy Spirit will make it possible that no one I know as well as myself, never will take the chip. It would be better to die, I say, than to take the chip. The desperation will not stop here, and that is why this will go on for several years as it will tighten and get worse. This is why Jerusalema is a refreshing song when you need to have some form of hope.

Another song that really resonated well with and for me that has enveloped the theme of the changing times was a song sang by Rudy Macre, a Scottish man. His song is titled Carry Us Over.

The label is of Big Stone Records by the producer Claude Sinclair (Big Stone). A powerful song that I need to go to one of the platforms and download.

This is not a promotion of the song, but the dynamics of this song reflects so much of the message in this book. Some parts of the words of song is actually in conflict with some of my views, nevertheless; still relevant. Besides, the image here is also to let you understand that whatever you choose to believe, Rudy Macre is actually a blood brother of us, and even though Esau, was established as our true enemy. The return of Yahua meant that we, the original Israelites were not held guiltless, and also we denied him when he returned, so now anyone and everyone is welcome to be a part of his Kingdom. Your race or ethnicity will not save you anymore.

Mark 16:16

15. And He said to them, "Go into the world and preach the gospel to every creature. 16. Whoever believes and is baptized will be saved, but whoever does not believe will be condemned."

Rudy Macre is my kindred spirit because his spiritual thoughts sit well with me, and this was one of the reasons why his song and even the sound of his music resonated with me.

I shall share with you some of his words.

'Carry us over Lord
This a Big Stone production
Carry us over Lord
Mi say a prayer for my leaders today
Give them strength and wisdom my Lord
Help them make the right decision
Right about now the world is in trouble

Andrew Beckford

All places shut

Don't watch the prices as they double My Lord

Mitzie say she will go to the back road and stand up

He will not recognize her in her clothes and make
up

Youths are crying

No food in the pot

Landlord forward, and he is not taking any chat

Garvey she works till her foot swell up

Stretching out the money but it still ain't adding up

Pressure building up she says the pipe will burst

Lord won't you plead our cause

That is why I am down on my knees

El Shaddai, won't you carry us please

Take the burden off my people shoulder

Daddy won't you carry us over Lord

Carry us over Lord

Carry us over

Carry us over Jah

Father all I want. All I need

Yes, we look to you

When the food runs out, the gas run out, and the
rent is well overdue

Right now my people hungry

Situation out a road it's kind of ugly

Won't believe me ask Ms Vicky

She tells you it is not pretty

For certain people opportunity

That is a scarce commodity

Oh father hear my plea

Send another Bogle, or another Sister Nanny,

Another Marcus Garvey Sam Sharpe or a Tacky

Lord send a Moses carry cross the Red Sea

Lord won't you hear my plea…' and it continues

This song is in fact, describing the tribulation that we are currently in.

Please download it because only then will you appreciate it.

It is also describing the birth pain, which means that it will only get worse, in fact, ten times worse. Therefore, I will say that all your plea is pointless because everyone on earth will face a harsher situation for several years, and many, many will die. I agree with his action because he is wise indeed, and it is the only way with evidence that we will know who is for and who is against him. Money is god for too many people and since they got the money, they completely change, but let us see what they will have to say now because the rich and famous will soon be on their knees, in fact everyone will be on their knees as they bow down to him and confess that Yahua Yahushua Messhiach is the Lord.

The last part of the song saying:

> **Send another Bogle, or another SisterNanny,**
> **Another Marcus Garvey Sam Sharpe or a Tacky**

Will never happen. What you need to ask him for, is for his return fast because that is what will happen. Yahua Yahushua Messhiach (Jesus Christ) shall return after the end of the tribulation, and no one knows the time or the hour he comes, but the signs are there, whereas; he himself said that if he never shorten the days, no flesh would be left on this earth. Let us be real, expect much worse to come. This is why the song Jerusalema is our only hope now as we prepare for his return to Jerusalem.

www.ingramcontent.com/pod-product-compliance
Lightning Source LLC
Chambersburg PA
CBHW021137130626
46554CB00005B/1541